THE
TECKMAN
BIOGRAPHY

Francis Durbridge

WILLIAMS AND WHITING

Cover design by Timo Schroeder

9781912582495

Williams & Whiting (Publishers)
15 Chestnut Grove, Hurstpierpoint,
West Sussex, BN6 9SS

Titles by Francis Durbridge published by Williams & Whiting

1   The Scarf – tv serial
2   Paul Temple and the Curzon Case – radio serial
3   La Boutique – radio serial
4   The Broken Horseshoe – tv serial
5   Three Plays for Radio Volume 1
6   Send for Paul Temple – radio serial
7   A Time of Day – tv serial
8   Death Comes to The Hibiscus – stage play
    The Essential Heart – radio play
    (writing as Nicholas Vane)
9   Send for Paul Temple – stage play

Murder At The Weekend – the rediscovered newspaper serials
and short stories

Also published by Williams & Whiting:
Francis Durbridge : The Complete Guide
By Melvyn Barnes

Titles by Francis Durbridge to be published by Williams &
Whiting
A Case For Paul Temple
A Game of Murder
A Man Called Harry Brent
A Time of Day
Bat Out of Hell
Breakaway – A Family Affair
Breakaway – The Local Affair
Melissa
Murder In The Media
My Friend Charles
One Man To Another – a novel

Paul Temple and the Alex Affair
Paul Temple and the Canterbury Case (film script)
Paul Temple and the Conrad Case
Paul Temple and the Geneva Mystery
Paul Temple and the Gilbert Case
Paul Temple and the Gregory Affair
Paul Temple and the Jonathan Mystery
Paul Temple and the Lawrence Affair
Paul Temple and the Madison Mystery
Paul Temple and the Margo Mystery
Paul Temple and the Spencer Affair
Paul Temple and the Sullivan Mystery
Paul Temple and the Vandyke Affair
Paul Temple and Steve
Paul Temple Intervenes
Portrait of Alison
Step In The Dark
The Desperate People
The Doll
The Other Man
The World of Tim Frazer
Three Plays for Radio Volume 2
Tim Frazer and the Salinger Affair
Tim Frazer and the Mellin Forrest Mystery
Twenty Minutes From Rome
Two Paul Temple Plays for Radio
Two Paul Temple Plays for Television

This book reproduces Francis Durbridge's original script together with the list of characters and actors of the BBC programme on the dates mentioned, but the eventual broadcast might have edited Durbridge's script in respect of scenes, dialogue and character names.

INTRODUCTION

Before considering the television serial *The Teckman Biography* it might be helpful to put Francis Durbridge (1912-98) in the context of his overall writing career, as by the time he launched into television in the 1950s he was already established as the foremost writer of mystery thrillers for BBC radio. As early as 1938 he had found the niche in which he was to make his name, when his radio serial *Send for Paul Temple* was so successful that it spawned sequels for thirty years that resulted in an enormous UK and European fanbase.

It was therefore natural that Durbridge, while continuing to write for radio, should join the rush of writers into the newer medium of television. In fact this was later clarified in a published interview (*Radio Times*, 21 October 1971) when he said: "Twenty years ago in the United States, a producer told me that I was wasting my time by not going into television. So that's what I did – I tried to build up a reputation with serials, since I'd vowed never to write a Paul Temple episode for television."

The result was *The Broken Horseshoe*, a six-episode serial transmitted by the BBC from 15 March to 19 April 1952, which entered the record books as the first thriller serial on British television whereas previously there had only been various series of thrillers in individual complete parts. In the light of this, C.A. Lejeune reviewed it in her *Observer* column (23 March 1952) in terms that now seem strange. She wrote: "It will be interesting to see how Mr. Durbridge manages his 're-capping' from week to week, for *The Broken Horseshoe* is a true serial and not a series of associated adventures with a beginning, middle and end. The skill with which such a programme can arrange for new viewers to start viewing here, without boring old viewers or wasting time, will achieve much to do with the serial's success. But if it goes on as well as it has begun, I don't intend to miss a Saturday." From this it appears that Durbridge was then regarded as an innovator, although he had been doing that very thing for over ten years on the radio!

The producer/director of *The Broken Horseshoe* was Martyn C. Webster, who had been Durbridge's regular producer on BBC radio since the 1930s. Indeed Webster was to remain as the producer/director of Durbridge's second BBC television serial *Operation Diplomat* (25 October to 29 November 1952), and he also directed the cinema film version of *The Broken Horseshoe* (Butchers/Nettlefold, 1953). But for Durbridge's third television serial *The Teckman Biography* the link with Webster was severed, although that partnership remained on radio for very many years until 1968. Instead *The Teckman Biography* (televised from 26 December 1953 to 30 January 1954 in six thirty-minute episodes) was produced and directed by Alvin Rakoff, with two changes to the episode titles in Durbridge's script – Episode 2, "A Letter of Introduction", was televised as "Charmaine"; and Episode 5, "Martin Teckman", as "The Man". This television serial was neither repeated nor released on DVD for the simple reason that (like its predecessors *The Broken Horseshoe* and *Operation Diplomat*) it was transmitted live and recordings have not been available.

After *The Teckman Biography* Francis Durbridge's television career blossomed and lasted for many years, from *Portrait of Alison* (16 February to 23 March 1955) to *Breakaway* (11 January to 28 March 1980). He built a solid reputation for teasing viewers with numerous red herrings, cliff-hanger endings to each episode, and the certainty that no character should be believed whatever they might say. As a result Durbridge's career in television drama was monumental, and this resulted in the unique recognition that for all his serials from 1960 (beginning with *The World of*

Tim Frazer) the BBC gave him the unprecedented accolade of the "*Francis Durbridge Presents*" screen credit before the title sequence of each episode.

In television's *The Teckman Biography* the leading man was the distinguished radio and television actor Patrick Barr, and he clearly impressed because he also became the protagonist in Durbridge's next television serial *Portrait of Alison*. But an interesting point is that Peter Coke, who played Maurice Miller in *The Teckman Biography*, became Durbridge's Paul Temple on BBC radio three months later and made the role very much his own in every Temple serial until they concluded in 1968. And in the small part of Walter, the cloakroom attendant, was James Beattie – who appeared as Paul Temple's cockney factotum Charlie in numerous radio serials from 1946 to 1963.

Not surprisingly *The Teckman Biography* was very quickly turned into a cinema film, given the fact that four movie versions of Durbridge's early Paul Temple radio serials and his first two television serials had proved popular. *The Teckman Mystery* (Corona/British Lion, 1954) was directed by Wendy Toye, with a screenplay by Durbridge and James Matthews, and there were many changes from the television original. Among the principal characters in the film there was no place for David Jefferies, while Chance's housekeeper Mrs Lacey was replaced by cheeky valet Leonard. The film's co-stars John Justin and Margaret Leighton, big cinema favourites in the 1950s, replaced television's Patrick Barr and Pamela Alan – which was the usual practice, as film producers tended to opt for proven cinema stars rather than television actors. And as always with Durbridge there was interest abroad, with the film *The Teckman Mystery* released for cinemas in Denmark as *Den farlige mand* and in Sweden as *Hemligheten F-109*, and dubbed on German television much later on 16 August 1960 as *Der Fall Teckmann*.

It is a delight to publish this original television script, as previously all we had was the cinema film. We can see in this, so much more than in the film, the skills of Francis Durbridge at a time when BBC Television was still finding its way and building its drama programming and reputation.

Melvyn Barnes
Author of *Francis Durbridge: The Complete Guide* (Williams & Whiting, 2018)

THE TECKMAN BIOGRAPHY

A serial in six episodes

By FRANCIS DURBRIDGE

Broadcast on BBC TV Dec 26th 1953 – Jan 30th 1954

CAST:

Philip Chance . . . . .Patrick Barr
Helen Teckman . . . . .Pamela Alan
Maurice Miller . . . . Peter Coke
Andrew Garvin . . . . .John Laurie
John Rice . . . . .Paul Whitsun-Jones
David Jefferies . . . .James Raglan
Detective-Inspector Hilton . Ivan Samson
Sergeant Blair . . . . Michael Bates
Drake . . . . Harry Towb
Stewardess . . . . .June Petersen
Walter . . . . James Beattie
Harold . . . .Harry Brunning
Man . . . . John Witty
Major Harris . . . . Anthony Nicholls
Betty . . . .Ann Murray
Joan . . . . Vera McKechnie
A Waiter . . . . Frank Pendlebury
Ruth Wade . . . . .Maureen Pryor
Sir Charles Shaughnessy . Peter Bathurst
Mrs. Lacey . . . . Margaret Boyd
Hector Briggs . . . . .Leslie Kyle
G.P.O. Messenger . . . . .Eddie Sutch
Waiter . . . . Stuart Nichol
Lydia . . . . Clare James

EPISODE ONE

THE PROPOSITION

OPEN TO: A row of beautifully bound volumes on a library shelf. A man's hand appears and takes down one of the books and opens it. The title page reads: "The Teckman Biography" by Francis Durbridge. The hand turns the page and the second page reads: Directed by Alvin Rakoff. The hand turns the page and we see a photograph of the actor playing PHILIP CHANCE: words, superimposed, state the name of the actor and character. The hand turns the page and we see a photograph of the actress playing the part of HELEN TECKMAN: words superimposed state the name of the character and actress. The hand turns the page. We read: Part One: The Proposition.

CUT TO: *A telephone on top of a writing bureau is ringing. A hand appears and lifts the phone. JOHN RICE is holding the telephone receiver. He is an American; stoutish; prosperous looking. He wears a dressing gown. We do not see DRAKE.*

RICE: Hello?

DRAKE: (*On the other end: an English voice*) John?

RICE: Yes.

DRAKE: (*Tensely*) We've found him!

RICE: Where?

DRAKE: He's in a café on the Tottenham Court Road.

RICE: Are you sure?

DRAKE: Yes …

RICE: (*Briskly*) Okay, you know what to do. Don't go in the café, wait until he comes out.

DRAKE: Right!

RICE: Ring me back!

RICE replaces the receiver.

CUT TO: *A YOUNG MAN is standing on a street corner. It is dark but there is a certain amount of light from a streetlamp. The YOUNG MAN is tall, slim, about thirty; wears horn-rimmed glasses and a camel hair overcoat. The overcoat is unfastened; the belt hanging loose. He is just about to cross the street when there is the sound of an approaching car. He hesitates; looks in the direction of the car. A beam of light sweeps from the car. Suddenly there is the sound of a revolver shot. The YOUNG MAN clutches his stomach and falls forward.*

CUT TO: *The telephone on the top of the writing bureau is ringing again. RICE, now wearing a lounge suit, picks up the receiver.*

RICE: Hello?

DRAKE: (*On the other end*) John?

RICE: Yes ...

DRAKE: Okay.

RICE: Right!

RICE still has his hand on the receiver although he has replaced it. He looks thoughtful; after a moment he lifts the receiver and dials.

RICE: (*On phone*) Continental Trunks? I want a call to Berlin ... Berlin 386411 ... Yes, a double one ... A personal call to a Mr Rudolph Kesner ... Kesner ... K-E-S-N-E-R ...

CUT TO: The Gentleman's Cloakroom at a popular café on the Tottenham Court Road.

WALTER, the attendant, is reading a novel; rows of hats and coats behind him. A MAN arrives and gives WALTER a ticket. WALTER rises and goes amongst the hats and coats. The MAN is tall, slim, about thirty. He wears horn-rimmed glasses. WALTER is searching amongst the hats and coats. He returns to the MAN.

WALTER: What did you have?

MAN: An overcoat.

WALTER: Just an overcoat?

MAN: (*Irritated*) Yes.

WALTER returns amongst the hats and coats. The man looking ill at ease; faintly on edge.

WALTER: (*Searching*) Well, that's very funny.

MAN: What do you mean?

WALTER: It doesn't appear to be here.

The MAN glances nervously around the café.

MAN: That doesn't strike me as being particularly funny.

WALTER: What time did you come in?

MAN: About half an hour ago.

WALTER:(*Passing the buck*) Ah – you must 'ave seen Leonard.

MAN: Quite possibly.

WALTER: What sort of a coat was it?

MAN: (*Annoyed*) It was a camel-hair coat, with a belt …

WALTER: (*Nodding*) We get a lot of those.

MAN: Well, do you think you could get mine?

WALTER continues the search.

WALTER: (*Suddenly*) Ah – here we are!

WALTER returns to the man and holds up a camel-hair overcoat. The MAN prepares to slip his arms through the sleeves. Suddenly he hesitates and takes hold of the coat.

MAN: (*Annoyed*) This isn't my coat!

WALTER: It isn't?

MAN: (*Angry*) No, it isn't!

WALTER gives a look of despair.

CUT TO: *RICE is packing a suitcase; there is a pile of shirts, socks, ties, etc., by the side of the case. There is the sound of a doorbell; he straightens up and goes and opens the door. DRAKE is standing in the doorway, he is a tough little man, fairly well dressed. At the moment he is obviously worried; a shade frightened.*

5

RICE: (*Surprised*) Drake! What the hell are you doing here? I told you not to come ...
DRAKE: John, I've got to see you!
RICE: What is it? What's happened?
DRAKE: We got the wrong man!

CUT TO: A shot of the open sky. A large airliner comes into shot.

CUT TO: An illuminated sign: FASTEN YOUR SEAT BELTS

CUT TO: The interior of an Aircraft. B.E.A. Elizabethan returning from the South of France. There is a full complement of passengers.
HELEN TECKMAN is sitting in a window seat next to PHILIP CHANCE. HELEN, a good-looking woman in her early thirties, is a reading a novel. She is on the last page. PHILIP is about forty-three or four; well-dressed; sophisticated; a faintly fastidious person. He is interested in the novel that HELEN is reading. Once or twice she looks up and catches his eye but he looks away. After a moment or two he surreptitiously looks across at the book again. The STEWARDESS walks down the plane and delivers a packet of cigarettes to one of the passengers. HELEN suddenly finishes reading and closes the book. PHILIP glances at her; she looks at him.
HELEN: (*Indicating the book*) Would you care to borrow it?
PHILIP: No, thank you. (*Smiling*) I have read it.
HELEN: You're sure? You didn't miss a page?
PHILIP: No, I – (*Suddenly laughing*) Oh, I see what you mean. No, I read it when it first came out. (*A moment*) Did you like it?
HELEN shakes her head.

6

PHILIP:	(*Surprised*) Oh? Why not?
HELEN:	I don't know. It seems rather a silly story. I liked that other book of his though. "Red Sky …
PHILIP:	"Red Sky All Day".
HELEN:	That's it. That was a wonderful book. I remember reading it at school and thinking …
PHILIP:	(*Taken aback*) At school?
HELEN:	Yes. Finishing school.
PHILIP:	Ah! (*Interested; pointing to the cover*) Tell me: why didn't you like this?
HELEN:	I think it's pretentious. I may be wrong of course. Obviously you didn't think so or …
PHILIP:	Ah, yes, but I'm afraid I don't count.
HELEN:	Why not? (*Puzzled*) What do you mean – you don't count?
PHILIP:	I wrote it.
HELEN:	You – (*Astonished*) Good Lord, are you Philip Chance?
PHILIP:	I'm afraid so.
HELEN:	But – (*She quickly picks up the book and looks at the back of the jacket*) But what a dreadful photograph! I'd never have recognised you.
PHILIP:	Yes, I'm afraid it's not very good.
HELEN:	It's terrible! You're much better looking than this.
PHILIP:	Thank you.
HELEN:	(*Faintly embarrassed*) I'm sorry I was rude just now.
PHILIP:	Rude?
HELEN:	About your book?
PHILIP:	Oh, that's all right. Anyway, you did like "Red Sky".
HELEN:	I adored it. We all did. The whole school.

7

PHILIP:	Even the Headmistress?
HELEN:	No, I don't think it got that far.
PHILIP:	I didn't think it would.

HELEN laughs.

PHILIP:	Have you been staying in Nice?
HELEN:	No; I've been staying at a place called Bandol.
PHILIP:	Where's that?
HELEN:	It's between Marseilles and Toulon.
PHILIP:	Oh, of course! I love the South of France, don't you?
HELEN:	The sunny place for shady people!
PHILIP:	(*Laughing*) Yes, I know. But I'm crazy about it. I've been three times this year.
HELEN:	Really?
PHILIP:	Yes, some friends of mine have a Villa just outside Antibes.
HELEN:	That must be heavenly.
PHILIP:	It's certainly convenient. (*A moment*) Do you live in London?
HELEN:	Yes, I've got a flat in Lowndes Square.
PHILIP:	Good Lord, so have I! Well – just around the corner, Hans Crescent.
HELEN:	We're practically neighbours.
PHILIP:	Yes …
HELEN:	Well, I shall certainly look forward to your next book, Mr Chance.
PHILIP:	Send a copy to your daughter – she'll probably be at finishing school by then.
HELEN:	(*Laughing*) I haven't got a daughter.

A pause.

PHILIP:	(*Looking at his watch*) Thank goodness we're on time. I'm supposed to be seeing my publisher at half-past four.

HELEN: I hope he'll bully you into writing another book.

PHILIP: He'll certainly try. Poor Maurice! I've been a bitter disappointment to him. Four novels in sixteen years. It's not exactly prolific, is it?

HELEN: I gather you don't like work.

PHILIP: Well, I must admit I prefer the South of France.

STEWARDESS: (*To PHILIP*) Would you mind fastening your belt, sir?

PHILIP: (*Nodding*) I think that's a very good idea.

PHILIP smiles at HELEN. The Fasten Your Seat Belts sign is illuminated.

CUT TO: The front door of PHILIP CHANCE's Flat. It has a small plaque with the name PHILIP CHANCE on it.

PHILIP arrives, wearing an overcoat, carrying a hat and suitcase. He puts down the suitcase, takes out a bunch of keys, and unlocks the door. He throws open the door and picks up the suitcase.

CUT TO: The Drawing Room of PHILIP's flat.

This is a very tastefully furnished room but at the moment it is in a state of complete chaos. The flat has obviously been burgled; the rooms ransacked.

PHILIP enters and suddenly stops dead. He drops the suitcase. He is staggered. He stares round the room then suddenly dashes into the bedroom. He returns almost immediately and crosses to the telephone which is on a small table. He picks up the receiver and dials 'O'.

PHILIP: Operator, get me the police! Yes … Yes, it's urgent!

CUT TO: *DETECTIVE-INSPECTOR HILTON examining the lock on the front door of PHILIP's flat. He is standing inside the flat; the door being open. He finishes his examination and slowly closes the door. PHILIP is in the drawing room watching the INSPECTOR who crosses to PHILIP.*

HILTON: Well, the lock hasn't been tampered with. Obviously, your visitor had a key.

PHILIP: (*Extremely irritated*) It's a pity he hadn't more imagination.

HILTON: What do you mean?

PHILIP: It seems absurd to turn the place upside down and overlook twenty-seven pounds and a gold cigarette case.

HILTON: Where did you say the money was?

PHILIP: In a drawer in the bedroom. I left it there before I went abroad. There was twenty-seven one-pound notes and a gold cigarette case.

HILTON: That's certainly very odd. (*Smiling*) Still, I shouldn't be annoyed because he hasn't taken anything, sir.

PHILIP: I'm damned annoyed about the whole business! Why pick on me?

HILTON: That's what they all say, sir!

SERGEANT BLAIR enters from the bedroom; he is carrying a small box.

PHILIP: Is there much of this sort of thing going on?

HILTON: Quite a bit, I'm afraid – especially in this neighbourhood.

PHILIP: (*Angry*) Well, can't you do anything about it?

HILTON: (*Nodding*) Don't worry, we've got our eye on the gentleman. (*To SERGEANT BLAIR*) Finished?

BLAIR: Yes, sir.

HILTON: Any luck?

BLAIR shakes his head.

PHILIP: That finger-print business seems a complete washout! Obviously if the fellow was clever

enough to get hold of a key, he was clever
enough to wear gloves.

BLAIR gives the INSPECTOR a 'look'.

BLAIR: They do slip up sometimes, sir.

PHILIP: (*Puzzled*) I just can't understand why he didn't take anything.

BLAIR holds out his hand; it contains a brass button.

BLAIR: Excuse me, sir – but does this belong to you?

PHILIP: (*Staring at the button*) What is it?

BLAIR: It's a button. I found it in the bedroom near the wardrobe.

PHILIP takes the button from SERGEANT BLAIR and examines it. It is a typical blazer button in shape; RAF wings engraved on it together with the numeral sixteen.

PHILIP: (*Handing the button over to the INSPECTOR*) No, I've never seen it before.

The front doorbell starts to ring.

HILTON: Looks as if it's been torn off a blazer. (*He examines the button*) Are you sure it isn't yours, sir?

PHILIP: Positive.

HILTON: (*Nodding*) All right, Sergeant, I'll take care of it. (*He puts the button in his pocket*)

The doorbell rings again.

BLAIR: (*To PHILIP*) Shall I see who that is, sir?

PHILIP: It's probably a Mr Miller. I'm expecting him.

SERGEANT BLAIR goes off. We hear the sound of the front door open.

BLAIR: (*Off*) Mr Miller?

MILLER: (*Off*) Yes.

BLAIR: (*Off*) You'd better come in, sir. Mr Chance is expecting you.

During the above:

HILTON: What time are you expecting your housekeeper back?

11

PHILIP: She's coming in tomorrow morning, about half past seven.

HILTON: Good. We'll have a word with her then.

MAURICE MILLER enters, followed by SERGEANT BLAIR. MILLER is a rather studious looking man in his early forties. He carries a manilla folder containing papers and photographs. He stares round the room in complete astonishment.

MILLER: Good God! What's going on here?

PHILIP: Hello, Maurice! Welcome to Casey's Court.

MILLER: But this is fantastic, old boy! What's happened?

PHILIP: Some damn fool broke in while I was away.

MILLER: Good Lord! What an unholy mess! Any idea who it was?

PHILIP: It certainly wasn't Raffles.

HILTON: (*To PHILIP; smiling*) We'll see you tomorrow morning, sir.

PHILIP: Yes, all right, Inspector.

HILTON: It's all right – we can let ourselves out.

BLAIR: Goodnight, sir.

PHILIP: Goodnight, Sergeant.

The INSPECTOR and the SERGEANT nod to MILLER and go out through the alcove. The sound of the front door opening and closing is heard.

MILLER: I say this is damn bad luck!

PHILIP: I was absolutely staggered when I walked in.

MILLER: (*Staring about him*) I can imagine it.

PHILIP: It's a jolly funny feeling, old boy. You can read about this sort of thing – you can even write about it – but when it happens to you …

MILLER: It's not so hot!

PHILIP: It certainly isn't! (*Nodding towards the door*) And those chaps! My God! Dead from the neck up …

12

MILLER: (*Laughing*) Philip, I know it's annoying, but the police can't work miracles.

PHILIP: No, I suppose not. But why pick on me for goodness sake – I haven't got a mink coat.

MILLER laughs.

PHILIP: Would you like a drink?

MILLER: It's a bit early for me.

PHILIP: Me too – but I'm having one.

MILLER: (*Laughing*) All right – I'll have a Scotch and soda.

PHILIP mixes the drinks and brings a drink to MILLER.

MILLER: Did you have a good holiday?

PHILIP: Oh, jolly good.

MILLER: I suppose you didn't do any work?

PHILIP: Don't be silly, old boy. (*He raises his glass*) Skoal!

MILLER raises his glass and drinks.

MILLER: Philip, we had a board meeting yesterday afternoon.

PHILIP: That must have been jolly.

MILLER: We had to make a decision about Barbara Jefferies.

PHILIP: What do you mean?

MILLER: Don't tell me you haven't heard about Barbara?

PHILIP: Has she written another book?

MILLER: She's had an accident, Philip. She's very ill – seriously ill.

PHILIP: Good heavens, really?

MILLER: She was knocked down by a car …

PHILIP: When?

MILLER: About three weeks ago. It was in all the papers. I'm surprised you didn't see it.

PHILIP: I never see the papers when I'm abroad – not if I can help it.

MILLER: Well, anyway, she's very ill – she's been on the danger list for almost a week.

PHILIP: I say, I am sorry.

MILLER: Anyway, Philip – the point is this. We'd asked Barbara to write a biography of Martin Teckman. She did a certain amount of research and then unfortunately the accident happened.

PHILIP: Go on …

MILLER: Well, I don't want to be pessimistic, but even if Barbara gets better it'll be a very long time before she'll do any writing. In any case, we particularly want to publish the book by the end of the year.

PHILIP: Why are you telling me all this?

MILLER: We want you to take over where Barbara Jefferies left off.

PHILIP: What?

MILLER: In other words – we want you to write the Teckman biography.

PHILIP: Are you crazy? I don't write biographies. I've never written one in my life. I'm a novelist.

MILLER: Yes, we know all that, Philip. If it comes to that Barbara's a novelist, she doesn't write biographies either. The point is, with this particular book we want a different approach. We don't just want the usual stereotyped biography.

PHILIP: Yes, but why come to me for Pete's sake?

MILLER: Because you're a writer, and a very good writer, and I'm quite sure that once you got interested in the subject, you'd turn out a first-class book.

PHILIP: But I don't know anything about Martin Teckman! He was a Test Pilot, wasn't he?

MILLER: That's right. He was killed about eighteen months ago.

PHILIP: Now what the devil do I know about Test Pilots?

MILLER: That's just the point. We don't want a book about Test Pilots – we want a book about Martin Teckman. Look Philip, there's plenty of people who

14

could write a book about Teckman, we know that. People who knew him, people he worked with – but we don't want that sort of book. I'm convinced that if the Teckman story is written by a writer – a creative writer – it'll be a best seller.

PHILIP: You may be right, Maurice. (*A shrug*) I don't know. Anyway, it's not my cup of tea.

MILLER: Look how Teckman was killed. He took the B.109 up for the first time. No one knew anything about the plane except that it was a hush-hush job. The thing disintegrated and Teckman was killed. Now if that isn't a rattling good story …

PHILIP: Look, Maurice, the only planes I'm interested in are the ones that fly to the South of France. And right now, I wish to God I was on one!

MILLER: (*Resigned*) All right, old boy.

PHILIP absently opens the folder, turns over the pages and glances at the photographs.

PHILIP: What's all this stuff?

MILLER: It's details about Teckman; biographical notes. I brought it along in case you were interested.

PHILIP: Oh. (*Looks at a photograph: suddenly*) I say, who's this?

MILLER takes the photograph from PHILIP and looks at it. It is a holiday photograph of HELEN TECKMAN on a country lawn; HELEN is in tweeds; there is a spaniel in the picture.

MILLER: (*Putting down the photograph*) Oh, that's Teckman's sister.

PHILIP: Why that's extraordinary!

MILLER: What do you mean?

PHILIP: She was on the plane this afternoon. I sat next to her.

MILLER: Really? (*Looks at the photograph*) She's a jolly good-looking girl.

15

PHILIP: Yes, she is. Do you know her?

MILLER: I've met her once or twice. (*Smiling*) Her name's Helen.

PHILIP: Maurice, why are you interested in Teckman anyway? Why do you want to do a book about him?

MILLER: I've told you why. I think it would make a rattling good biography. Besides … (*Suddenly*) Look, Philip – do me a favour. Don't reject this idea, not yet at any rate. Read this stuff through, then if you're interested go and have a talk to Andrew Garvin.

PHILIP: (*Looking down at the papers in the folder*) Who's Andrew Garvin?

MILLER: He was a friend of Teckman's; they worked together on the B.109. He's a crazy old boy but he was devoted to Teckman, knows more about him than anybody.

PHILIP: Does he live in Town?

MILLER: No, he's got a cottage in Hertfordshire somewhere.

PHILIP picks up the photograph of HELEN TECKMAN again; he studies it for a moment and then thoughtfully puts it down on the table.

PHILIP: (*Thoughtfully*) All right, Maurice, I'll tell you what I'll do. I'll read this stuff …

MILLER: (*Pleased*) Good …

PHILIP: … Then if I'm interested, I'll have a talk to Garvin.

MILLER: Jolly good!

PHILIP: But I warn you, this doesn't mean I'm going to write the book.

MILLER: No, of course not.

(*MILLER smiles*)

CUT TO: A country lane in Hertfordshire.

A car drives up to a small detached cottage. It stops and PHILIP gets out of it and walks through the wicket gate and down the garden path to the front door of the cottage. He knocks on the front door.

CUT TO: The interior of ANDREW GARVIN's cottage.

ANDREW GARVIN opens the door and faces PHILIP. GARVIN is a pipe-smoking, thickset, untidy Scotsman in his middle sixties. He wears grey flannel 'bags', and a cardigan.

PHILIP: Mr Garvin?

GARVIN: Aye …

PHILIP: I telephoned from London. My name's Chance.

GARVIN: Oh, yes – come in, Mr Chance. I'm afraid I didn't catch your name over the phone.

PHILIP enters the main room of the cottage. There is a mass of books, newspapers, pipe-racks, worn chairs and a settee. There are several photographs on an old-fashioned sideboard together with a model of the B.109., large decanter of whisky, two bottles of Scotch and a soda syphon.

GARVIN: Take a pew – if you can find one.

PHILIP: Thank you.

GARVIN: (*Taking a pouch from his pocket*) I'm afraid I can't offer you a cigarette. Do you smoke a pipe?

PHILIP: No, thank you.

GARVIN: (*Pointing to the armchairs*) So you're going to write a book about Martin Teckman?

PHILIP: Well, yes, I think so …

PHILIP sits in one of the armchairs: GARVIN on the arm of the one opposite.

GARVIN: I thought a woman called Barbara Jefferies was going to write this book. I had a note from her; she made an appointment to see me, but the lassie never turned up.

17

PHILIP: No; unfortunately, she was involved in a motor car accident; she's still in hospital.

GARVIN: Oh, I'm sorry to hear that.

PHILIP: (*Leaning forward*) Mr Garvin, I understand that you were a personal friend of Teckman's.

GARVIN: That's true, I was.

PHILIP: When did you first meet him?

GARVIN: In 1942, yes – February, '42. I was the technical Assistant to the Director of Experimental Aircraft. We were stationed at Tewkesbury and Martin was sent down there by one of the Ministries. He was very annoyed because he wanted to go into the RAF and they just wouldn't take him.

PHILIP: Why not?

GARVIN: They thought he was more useful to us at Tewkesbury; an' they were dead right – he was.

PHILIP: That was in '42.

GARVIN: Yes.

PHILIP: How old was he then?

GARVIN: Oh, twenty-two or three …

PHILIP: Very young …

GARVIN: Very. But he was a brilliant lad; he'd already taken a Science degree and he'd had eighteen months with Walters-Armitage.

PHILIP: What did he do exactly, at Tewkesbury, I mean?

GARVIN: Well, for the first six months he was in the drawing office, but we could see that wasn't going to work out, so we transferred him to the experimental station. He had a brain like blotting paper; he just absorbed everything – in next to no time he knew more about the mathematical side of aircraft production than any of us.

PHILIP: Was he a studious type?

18

GARVIN: Not in appearance; he was a fine-looking chap; the girls were crazy about him.

PHILIP: And was he crazy about the girls?

GARVIN: M'm – up to a point. But he could never quite bring himself down to their level. (*Amused*) If he took a girl to a dance likely as not, he'd talk about nuclear fission most of the night. (*Crossing to the sideboard*) But have you never seen a photograph of Martin?

PHILIP: No, I don't think I have.

GARVIN picks up a photograph off the sideboard and returns to PHILIP with it.

GARVIN: (*Showing PHILIP the photograph*) Well, this was taken just after he left Tewkesbury – about a week before he joined the RAF. (*Pointing*) That's his sister …

PHILIP: Oh, is it? I didn't recognise her.

GARVIN: No, it's not a very good one of Helen, I think she moved when the picture was being taken. (*Taking the photograph back to the sideboard*) Do you know Helen Teckman?

PHILIP: Yes, curiously enough we have met, but it was just a coincidence. She doesn't know I'm interested in her brother.

GARVIN: (*Looking at PHILIP*) I see.

PHILIP: We met on a plane coming back from the South of France.

GARVIN: (*Nodding*) She seems to travel about quite a lot these days. She's a curious girl.

PHILIP: A jolly good-looking one.

GARVIN: (*Thoughtfully*) Aye – I suppose she is …

PHILIP: When did Teckman leave Tewkesbury and join the RAF?

19

GARVIN: In '44. We were very annoyed about the whole business. He didn't say a word to anybody; he simply volunteered, and the fools accepted him. When he was demobbed, he applied for a job as a Test Pilot with Walters-Armitage. They were delighted, of course.

PHILIP: Did you see much of him – after he was demobbed?

GARVIN crosses to the decanter of whisky on the sideboard and pours himself a liberal helping of neat whisky.

GARVIN: Oh, quite a bit. He stayed with me for three or four months. You see, I was with Walters myself, working on the B.109.

PHILIP: I see. Are you still with them?

GARVIN: No, I retired about a year ago. We didn't quite see eye to eye.

GARVIN returns to PHILIP and stands looking down at him.

GARVIN: Young man, am I the first person you've seen, about this book, I mean?

PHILIP: Yes, my publisher – Maurice Miller – said you knew more about Teckman than anybody.

GARVIN: Maybe he's right. But I think I ought to warn you. I'm not considered a very reliable source of information these days.

PHILIP: What do you mean?

GARVIN: If you pursue these investigations sooner, or later you'll meet Sir Charles Shaughnessy. He's the big noise. The head of Walters-Armitage.

PHILIP: Well?

GARVIN: He'll tell you not to believe a word I say. He'll tell you I'm a fool, a charlatan, and a dipsomaniac.

PHILIP: And are you?

GARVIN: (*Smiling*) A fool – perhaps. A charlatan – no. A dipsomaniac – (*Nodding*) Yes. (*He drinks*)

A pause.

PHILIP: Mr Garvin, how important was the B.109?

GARVIN: (*Putting down his empty glass*) How important?

PHILIP: Yes.

GARVIN: Are you a scientist?

PHILIP: No.

GARVIN: Do you know anything about aircraft production? About light alloys? About the theory of central vibration?

PHILIP: No, nothing.

GARVIN: (*A shrug*) Then how can I answer your question? How important was the first motor car? The first tank? The first atom bomb?

PHILIP: All right, I'll put my question another way? How important was Martin Teckman's work on the B.109?

GARVIN: (*Turning; suddenly angry*) More important than those damned stiff-shirted fools up at Walters ever realised! Martin ought never to have flown that plane. I told Shaughnessy; I told Shaughnessy the night before the test, but the fool wouldn't listen.

PHILIP: You mean, you knew there was going to be an accident?

GARVIN: (*Turning away; shaking his head*) No. No, that's not what I meant. (*Changes the subject*) Have you ever seen a model of the B.109?

GARVIN crosses to the sideboard and picks up the model of the B.109.

PHILIP: No.

GARVIN: (*Returning to PHILIP with the model*) Well, here we are.

PHILIP takes the model and examines it with interest.

GARVIN: If you'd like a photograph for your book, you're very welcome.

21

PHILIP: Thank you. (*Examining the model*) Did you make this?

GARVIN: No, Martin made it – that's why I suggested the photograph.

PHILIP: It's a very good idea.

PHILIP returns the model to GARVIN who returns it to the sideboard.

PHILIP: (*Puzzled*) Mr Garvin, what did you mean when you said that you warned Sir Charles Shaughnessy?

GARVIN: I told him that Martin ought not to fly the B.109.

PHILIP: Why? Didn't you think the plane was ready?

GARVIN: (*Looking at his pipe, pressing the tobacco*) The plane was ready.

PHILIP: Then – you had your doubts about Teckman?

GARVIN: He was physically fit; dead keen; the best pilot they had.

PHILIP: Well, then …?

GARVIN: Mr Chance, you're an intelligent, imaginative man. You read about the accident?

PHILIP: Yes.

GARVIN: Well – what do you think happened?

PHILIP: But we know what happened! The plane disintegrated and Teckman was killed.

GARVIN: Where?

PHILIP: Well, they said it happened over the North Sea. Didn't they find part of the plane, part of the fuselage?

GARVIN: (*Taking out an old-fashioned cigarette lighter; nodding*) Aye, they did. They found it and they brought it back to Walters, back to Sir Charles and his distinguished looking colleagues. Oh, there was no doubt about it, it was part of the B.109 all

22

	right. Everybody said so, everybody was convinced – Well … nearly everybody.
PHILIP:	You mean – you don't think it was?
GARVIN:	No …
PHILIP:	(*Staring at him*) You don't think the plane did disintegrate?
GARVIN:	(*Emphatically*) No, I don't …
PHILIP:	But the fuselage?
GARVIN:	I think what they found had been very carefully planted …
PHILIP:	(*Incredulously*) Then what happened to the B.109?

GARVIN looks at PHILIP; flicks his lighter and lights his pipe. He is still looking at PHILIP.

GARVIN: It landed somewhere …

CUT TO: The Front Door of PHILIP CHANCE's flat.

A POSTMAN arrives; stops in front of the door; glances through a pile of letters he is carrying. He drops several letters through the letterbox and then departs. DETECTIVE-INSPECTOR HILTON arrives; he rings the doorbell and stands waiting for the door to be opened. After a pause he rings the doorbell again. The door is opened by PHILIP; he is wearing a dressing-gown; holds a letter in his hand which he has obviously been reading.

HILTON: Good morning, sir!

PHILIP: Oh, hello, Inspector!

HILTON: (*Smiling*) Sorry if I'm too early for you, sir.

PHILIP: Not at all. I thought it was my housekeeper. Come in, Inspector!

HILTON follows PHILIP into the flat.

CUT TO: The Drawing Room of PHILIP's flat.

PHILIP and HILTON enter. The room is now quite normal; everything tidy and in its correct position.

HILTON: Well, it hasn't taken you long to get straight, sir.

PHILIP: The bedroom's still in a bit of a mess. Well – any developments, Inspector?

HILTON: Yes, we picked up the gentleman I was telling you about.

PHILIP: Did you, by Jove! That's quick work.

HILTON: Yes, but unfortunately we don't seem to have got anywhere. He admits he did a job on the Brompton Road and two in Lowndes Square, but he swears he didn't touch this place.

PHILIP: Well, obviously the fellow's lying.

HILTON: I don't think so, sir. After all, there's no reason why he should lie. He didn't take anything from here and we've booked him, anyway.

PHILIP: Yes, that's true.

HILTON: (*Taking the button from his pocket*) Mr Chance, have you got any friends who were in the RAF during the war?

PHILIP: Good heavens, yes. Who hasn't?

HILTON: In the 16th Squadron?

PHILIP: (*Looks a shade puzzled*) Oh, good Lord, I wouldn't know about that. I haven't a clue as to what Squadron they were in. Why do you ask?

HILTON: This button rather intrigued me. I've checked the number on it. There was a 16th Squadron. It was stationed in Hertfordshire part of the time: attached to Fighter Command.

The telephone starts to ring.

PHILIP: Well, where does that get us?

HILTON: (*Looking at the button in his hand; thoughtfully*) I don't know, sir.

24

PHILIP crosses to the telephone.

PHILIP: Excuse me, Inspector.

HILTON: Do you mind if I have another look in the bedroom, sir?

PHILIP: No, of course not. Go ahead.

INSPECTOR HILTON goes into the bedroom. PHILIP answers the phone.

PHILIP: Hello? … Yes … Yes, speaking … Who? … Oh, Mr Rice! Curiously enough I was just reading your letter … Yes, well my agent usually handles that sort of thing, can't you … I beg your pardon? … Well – what sort of a proposition is it? (*Looks at the letter*) No, you don't say, you simply say that you've read a book of mine, and that you … Yes, that's right … Yes, I did … I beg your pardon? … Yes, I could probably do that … All right then, let's meet for a drink. Do you know The Storey Club, Carlton House Terrace? … That's it – that's the place … Half-past twelve? … Right … I'll see you then. Goodbye.

PHILIP replaces the receiver and then looks again at the letter.

CUT TO: The Storey Club, Carlton House Terrace.

HAROLD, the Steward, is reading a letter. He is in his office-cum-cubby hole. There is a door leading to the Smoking Room and another door into the street. Letters, notices etc are attached to a noticeboard. HAROLD wears a uniform and service ribbons. DAVID JEFFERIES enters from the street. He is a tall, rather angular-looking man. HAROLD rises.

HAROLD: Good morning, sir!

JEFFERIES: Good morning, Harold.

HAROLD: I've got a book for you, sir. Major Claygate left it.

JEFFERIES: Ah, yes!

HAROLD takes a book from a cubby hole and hands it to JEFFERIES.

HAROLD: I think this is the one, sir.

JEFFERIES: (*Looking at the title*) Yes, that's right.

HAROLD: How's Mrs Jefferies, sir?

JEFFERIES: Oh – she's a little better, Harold. Thank you.

PHILIP CHANCE enters from the street. He wears a homburg hat and carries a walking stick.

PHILIP: (*Taking off his hat*) Why, hello, Jefferies!

JEFFERIES: (*Turning*) Hello, Chance! When did you get back?

PHILIP: Monday afternoon. I say, I was terribly sorry to hear about your wife.

JEFFERIES: Yes, it's pretty grim, isn't it?

PHILIP: I didn't know anything about it until Maurice told me.

JEFFERIES: Maurice was very upset.

PHILIP: Is there any news?

JEFFERIES: Well, she was a little better last night. I'm keeping my fingers crossed.

PHILIP: Oh, good.

JEFFERIES: Did Maurice speak to you about the book?

PHILIP: The biography? Yes, he did as a matter of fact. I'm very interested. I shall probably write it.

JEFFERIES: (*Nodding*) Well, I wish you luck. I wish to God Barbara had stuck to novels; she'd have probably been all right if she had have done.

PHILIP: What do you mean? She was knocked down by a car, wasn't she?

JEFFERIES: That's right. She walked out of the house one night – she had an appointment to see a friend of Teckman's – a car came round the corner

26

> and, well – it was all over in a matter of seconds.

PHILIP shakes his head.

JEFFERIES: The swine didn't even stop.

PHILIP: No, really?

JEFFERIES: (*Nodding*) Still I don't suppose it would have made any difference to Barbara if he had have done. Well, I must be off!

PHILIP: Goodbye, Jefferies!

JEFFERIES: Goodbye.

PHILIP: Give my love to Barbara when you see her.

JEFFERIES: I will, certainly.

JEFFERIES goes.

PHILIP: (*To HAROLD*) I'm expecting a Mr Rice, Harold. I'd be grateful if …

HAROLD: He is in the Smoking Room, sir – he arrived about five minutes ago.

PHILIP: Oh, thank you.

CUT TO: A corner of the Smoking Room.

PHILIP enters and looks round the room. RICE rises from an armchair; he smiles at PHILIP and holds out his hand.

RICE: Mr Chance?

PHILIP: Yes.

RICE: I'm John Rice. Delighted to know you, Mr Chance.

They shake hands.

RICE: It's very nice of you to spare me a few moments.

PHILIP: I'm sorry I'm late, I didn't realise …

RICE: That's all right. You're a very busy man. I appreciate that.

PHILIP beckons towards the armchair. They both sit.

PHILIP: Would you care for a drink?

RICE: Not just at the moment, if you don't mind. Mr
            Chance, I've just finished reading a book of yours.
            Red Sky All Day.

PHILIP nods.

RICE: I enjoyed it enormously.

PHILIP: Thank you.

RICE: I was particularly interested in the last two
            chapters; the Berlin sequence. I gather you know
            Berlin pretty well.

PHILIP: I did before the war. I haven't been there since
            '36.

RICE: Well, now that's interesting. Not since '36?

PHILIP: No.

RICE: It's changed, you know.

PHILIP: (*Smiling*) Yes, I rather imagine it has.

RICE: Have you ever thought of going back there?

PHILIP: Why, no. Why should I?

RICE: Mr Chance, I've got a proposition to make to you.
            But first of all, let me tell you who I am and what I
            am. I represent an American magazine called "The
            New World". I don't suppose you've ever heard   of
            it because it isn't on the bookstalls yet.

PHILIP: When you say you represent the magazine …

RICE: I'm the European representative and I'm also on
            the board of directors. We're a five-million-dollar
            outfit – however, that's neither here nor there. Now
            our proposition is this. We want you to go to Berlin
            and write a series of articles for us.

PHILIP: What kind of articles? Political or …

RICE: No, no, no, we don't want anything political. We
            just want you to mix with the Berliners. Tell us what
            sort of food Mrs Schmidt is eating, how much her
            husband pays for his suits, what kind of shows they

28

	like, what sort of books they read. We want a completely frank picture of life in Berlin.
PHILIP:	I take it you mean the Western Zone?
RICE:	(*Laughing*) Oh, sure – we're not asking you to go into the Eastern Zone.
PHILIP:	Well – (*Suddenly laughing*) You know, this is a completely different proposition from what I expected. I thought you were going to ask me to write a film.
RICE:	Well – what do you say?
PHILIP:	But – how do you know I can write the sort of stuff you want?
RICE:	I read your book.
PHILIP:	It's a long time since I wrote that book.
RICE:	Okay, it's a long time. So what? Maybe you've improved?
PHILIP:	Is this a definite offer?
RICE:	Sure. (*Puzzled*) Doesn't the proposition interest you?
PHILIP:	Yes, it interests me, but …
RICE:	But what?
PHILIP:	I can't accept.
RICE:	Why not?
PHILIP:	Well, for one thing I've made up my mind to write a book, and secondly …
RICE:	What sort of a book – a novel?
PHILIP:	No, a biography. I'm going to write the biography of a man called Martin Teckman.
RICE:	(*Quietly*) I see.
PHILIP:	Have you heard of him?
RICE:	Sure, I've heard of him. He was a Test Pilot.
PHILIP:	That's right.
RICE:	Tell me: have you signed a contract for this thing? Is it all tied up?

PHILIP: No, not yet, but –

RICE: Well, what are you worrying about? Look – we want you to go to Berlin for six months. During those six months we want you to write six articles; three thousand words each, eighteen thousand words altogether. We'll pay all travel, hotel expenses, and give you three hundred dollars a week to play around with. On top of which we'll pay you twenty-one hundred dollars an article …

PHILIP: (*Amazed*) Twenty-one hundred dollars!

RICE: That's right. If you want it in sterling, that's seven hundred and fifty pounds an article. Four thousand five hundred pounds altogether.

PHILIP: (*Amazed*) Why – that's extraordinarily generous!

RICE: There's one condition.

PHILIP: What's that?

RICE: If we like your articles, we should want an option on your services for another six months, in which case we should probably send you down to Monte Carlo.

PHILIP: Monte Carlo?

RICE: Yes. We're thinking of doing some articles on the Riviera.

PHILIP: That's an excellent idea!

RICE: You know the sort of thing – "Europe's Playground. Typist Meets Millionaire!"

PHILIP: I know exactly the sort of thing!

RICE: (*A gesture*) Well – there you are – that's the proposition.

PHILIP: (*After a tiny pause*) Mr Rice, when would you want me to leave?

RICE: For Berlin?

PHILIP: Yes.

RICE: Monday. Well, Tuesday at the latest. If you
           accept I suggest we meet again tomorrow, and I'll
           give you your ticket and an advance of – say, a
           thousand pounds.
PHILIP: (*Suddenly: delighted; holding out his hand*) It's a
           deal!
RICE: Okay! (*Shaking hands*) Now, if you don't mind,
           we'll have that drink.

PHILIP laughs.

CUT TO: The Entrance Hall of the Club.

*HAROLD is in his cubby-hole-cum-office reading the evening
paper. MAURICE MILLER comes through the main door.
HAROLD lowers his newspaper.*

HAROLD: Oh, good evening, sir!

MILLER: Good evening, Harold!

HAROLD: I've got a registered letter for you, sir. It arrived
           by the afternoon post.

*HAROLD takes the letter from a drawer and hands it to
MILLER. He also produces a stiff-backed exercise book.*

MILLER: Oh, thank you. (*He takes the letter and puts it in his
pocket*)

HAROLD: Would you mind signing the book, Mr Miller?

MILLER: Certainly.

*HAROLD offers MILLER a pen and MILLER signs his name in
the book. PHILIP walks into the hall carrying his hat and
walking stick.*

MILLER: (*Turning*) Oh, hello, Philip! I've been trying to get
           hold of you. I telephoned you three times this
           morning but there was no reply.

PHILIP: Yes, I've been out most of the day.

MILLER: Did you read that stuff I left you?

PHILIP: I did, and I was very interested. I even went down to
           see Garvin.

MILLER: (Delighted) Did you, by Jove! Jolly good! (Laughing) He's quite a character, isn't he?

PHILIP: He certainly is!

MILLER: (Very pleased) Well, I thought you'd change your mind, Philip, once you had the opportunity of …

PHILIP: (Interrupting) Maurice, I'm sorry – it's no good.

MILLER: What do you mean?

PHILIP: I'm not going to write that book.

MILLER: (Amazed) You're not!

PHILIP: No.

MILLER: But why? I thought you said that …

PHILIP: I've accepted another offer, Maurice. I'm leaving for Berlin, on Tuesday.

MILLER: Berlin!

PHILIP: Yes.

MILLER: Well – there's nothing more to be said.

PHILIP: I'm afraid not. (A moment) I'm sorry, Maurice. I'd like to have written the book – believe me I would – but this offer is too good, I just can't turn it down.

MILLER: Well, if it's as good at that.

PHILIP: It is, old boy – really it is.

MILLER: What is it – a film?

PHILIP: No; I'm going to write some magazine articles. Lots of filthy lucre and very little work.

MILLER: They've got the right man!

PHILIP laughs.

MILLER: All right, Philip. You can't say I didn't try. (He pats PHILIP's shoulder) Have a good trip – take care of yourself.

PHILIP: Thanks a lot! Goodbye.

PHILIP gives a friendly little wave and goes out.

32

CUT TO: The Front Door of PHILIP's flat.

PHILIP arrives; he is very pleased with himself; quite gay; whistling. He takes his keys out of his pocket; tosses them up and down; unlocks the door and lets himself into the flat.

CUT TO: Inside the flat.

PHILIP enters; tosses his hat and stick down; crosses to the bedroom door, then stops dead. He stares in amazement. The dead body of ANDREW GARVIN is sprawled on the floor in front of the bedroom door. He is clutching the model of the B.109.

END OF EPISODE ONE

EPISODE TWO

A LETTER OF INTRODUCTION

Open to: A hand takes a book from the shelf and pages turn. The camera focuses on a certain page which reads:

PHILIP CHANCE, a novelist, is asked to write the biography of Martin Teckman, a test pilot whose plane disintegrated on its first flight. To learn more about the subject, PHILIP interviews ANDREW GARVIN who worked with Teckman on the B.109. Later, when Philip returns to his flat, he finds the body of Andrew Garvin. In Garvin's hand is a model of the B.109.

CUT TO: The Drawing Room of PHILIP CHANCE's flat.

The body of ANDREW GARVIN and the model of the B.109. PHILIP is staring down at the body in astonishment. He stoops down and is about to pick up the model; he suddenly hesitates, then changes his mind. He turns towards the telephone and dials a number.

PHILIP: (*On phone*) Hello? … Oh – I want to speak to Inspector Hilton. (*A pause*) Hello? … Inspector? This is Philip Chance. I – want you to come round to my flat straight away … Yes, it's very urgent. (*Tensely*) Well – someone's been murdered … Yes, of course … All right.

PHILIP replaces the receiver and then doesn't quite know what to do; he looks round the room; takes out a cigarette case and lights a cigarette. A sudden thought occurs to him and he lifts the telephone receiver and dials.

PHILIP: (*After a moment. On phone*) Hello? … Harold? … This is Mr Chance … Is Mr Miller still in the Club? … Well, listen, Harold – I want you to deliver a message for me. Tell Mr Miller to jump into a cab and come round to my flat straightaway … Yes … Thank you, Harold.

PHILIP replaces the receiver then puts the cigarette in his mouth; he looks worried and very serious.

CUT TO: The Drawing Room of PHILIP's flat.

INSPECTOR HILTON is examining the body of ANDREW GARVIN; he has turned the body over on its side; he lets the body fall back into position then, using his handkerchief, picks up the model of the B.109. He straightens up. SERGEANT BLAIR and PHILIP are watching him.

PHILIP: How long do you think he's been dead?

HILTON: (*Looking at PHILIP*) Some little time. We'll see what the doctor says …

PHILIP: How was he killed, do you know?

HILTON: Don't you know, Mr Chance?

PHILIP: No, of course I don't. I didn't examine the body.

HILTON: He was knifed – stabbed, if you prefer the word.

PHILIP: But – if he was stabbed – where's the knife?

HILTON: Where, indeed? It certainly isn't here.

PHILIP: (*Suddenly*) Look here, Inspector – you don't think I had anything to do with this?

HILTON: (*Ignores the remark – looks at the model*) Did you touch this?

PHILIP: No, I've told you – I didn't touch anything – except the telephone.

HILTON: (*To SERGEANT BLAIR*) Well, there's prints on it – you'd better set to work.

BLAIR: Yes, sir.

HILTON: (*To BLAIR*) Take it down to the Yard and tell Carver and Fagan I want them. I definitely want pictures before the doctor gets here.

BLAIR: Yes, sir.

BLAIR takes the model and goes out.

HILTON: You say his name is Garvin – Andrew Garvin?

PHILIP: Yes.

HILTON: Well – what happened?

PHILIP: I don't know what happened.

HILTON: Tell me what you do know, Mr Chance.

PHILIP: On Monday afternoon, my publisher, a man called
          Maurice Miller, asked me to write a book for him –
          a biography of a man called Martin Teckman.

HILTON: The Test Pilot?

PHILIP: Yes. He told me to have a chat with a friend of
          Teckman's called Andrew Garvin. I went down to
          see Garvin yesterday afternoon.

HILTON: Go on.

PHILIP: Garvin told me quite a lot about Teckman and he
          showed me the model of the B.109, the plane that
          Teckman was flying when he was killed. He
          suggested that since Teckman had made the
          model it might be a very good idea to have it
          photographed.

HILTON: Why?

PHILIP: Well, he thought I might want to use the
          photograph in the book I was writing.

HILTON: I see. Go on.

PHILIP: I said goodbye to Garvin and came back to Town.

HILTON: That was yesterday afternoon?

PHILIP: Yes. This morning – after you left – I did some
          shopping and then went to my Club.

HILTON: Which Club?

PHILIP: The Storey Club, Carlton House Terrace. I left the
          Club at about three o'clock, arrived home at about a
          quarter to four. When I got here – I found Garvin.

HILTON: I take it several people saw you this afternoon, at
          the Club I mean?

PHILIP: Yes, of course they did. I had an appointment with
          a Mr Rice, Inspector …

HILTON: Yes?

PHILIP: What happens in a case of this kind?

HILTON: What do you mean, sir?

PHILIP: Well, I'm supposed to be leaving for Berlin on Tuesday and I shouldn't like …

HILTON: (*Interrupting*) Berlin?

PHILIP: Yes.

HILTON: In connection with the biography?

PHILIP: No; I've changed my mind. I've had an offer to go to Berlin and write some magazine articles.

HILTON: I see. So there was really no necessity for you to see Garvin yesterday afternoon?

PHILIP: No, I suppose there wasn't, except that at the time I intended to write the book.

HILTON: (*Quite calmly*) But you changed your mind?

PHILIP: Yes.

HILTON: Why?

PHILIP: (*Faintly rattled*) I've told you why. I received another offer.

HILTON: I see. (*Nods; there is a pause*) May I use your telephone?

PHILIP: Yes, of course.

HILTON: Have you an extension?

PHILIP: Yes, in the bedroom.

HILTON: Thank you.

HILTON goes into the bedroom. The doorbell rings. PHILIP goes into the hall and opens the front door. MILLER is standing outside.

PHILIP: Hello, Maurice. Thank goodness you got here.

MILLER: Philip, what is it? I got your message just as I was leaving the Club. What's happened?

PHILIP: Garvin's dead.

MILLER: Garvin?

PHILIP: Yes.

MILLER: You mean Andrew Garvin?

PHILIP: Yes. He's been murdered.

MILLER: Murdered? But Philip …

PHILIP: He's in here.

MILLER: In here?

PHILIP: Come in.

PHILIP beckons MILLER into the drawing room. MILLER stares down at the body of ANDREW GARVIN. He is obviously bewildered.

MILLER: I say. This is terrible. When did it happen?

PHILIP: I don't know. I don't even know what he was doing here.

MILLER: You mean – you just found him – in the flat?

PHILIP: Yes. I came back from the Club, and – well – there he was.

MILLER: Have you sent for the police?

PHILIP: Yes, the Inspector's already here; he's in the bedroom, telephoning.

MILLER: Why did you send for me?

PHILIP: (*A shade angry*) Why did I send for you? You introduced me to Garvin, if it hadn't been for you …

MILLER: Now wait a minute, Philip! I didn't exactly introduce you to him. I told you that he'd be well worth interviewing.

PHILIP: Yes, well I wish to goodness I'd never listened to you! (*Facing MILLER; a shade exasperated*) Maurice, there's something I don't like about this Teckman business. Something I don't understand.

MILLER: What do you mean?

PHILIP: Barbara Jefferies decides to write the biography of Martin Teckman and within a matter of weeks she's knocked down by a car and very nearly killed. I then get interested in the proposition and within twenty-four hours the first person I interview is murdered.

MILLER: That's just a coincidence, Philip, you can't …

41

PHILIP: Well, it's the sort of coincidence I'm not mad about.

MILLER: (*Seriously*) You don't really think the Teckman business has got anything to do with this?

PHILIP: Yes, I do. And there's another thing, Maurice. My flat was burgled; remember, the whole place was turned upside down.

MILLER: Well?

PHILIP: Well, is that just another coincidence?

MILLER: But that happened while you were in the South of France, before I even discussed the Teckman proposition with you.

PHILIP: (*Thoughtfully*) Yes, I know, but –

MILLER: But what?

PHILIP: The police found a button in my bedroom; it had been torn off a blazer. It had Wings on it. R.A.F. Wings …

MILLER: Well?

PHILIP: (*Slowly*) Martin Teckman was in the R.A.F.

HILTON comes out of the bedroom.

MILLER: Good heavens, Philip! So was I, so were thousands of other people. You're not seriously suggesting that … (*He stops on seeing HILTON*)

HILTON: (*Quietly*) Good afternoon, Mr Miller.

MILLER: Oh, good afternoon, Inspector.

PHILIP: (*To HILTON*) I sent for Miller; he can confirm what I've already told you.

HILTON: (*Smiling; almost patronisingly*) I'm quite sure he can, Mr Chance. (*He looks down at GARVIN, then across to MAURICE MILLER*) Did you know Garvin?

MILLER: (*Hesitant*) Yes, we met about eight or nine years ago.

HILTON: Where?

42

MILLER: In Oxford. I went there with a friend – or rather, an acquaintance. He introduced us.

HILTON: Was your acquaintance a friend of Garvin's?

MILLER: Yes.

HILTON: What was his name?

MILLER: (*After a pause*) Martin Teckman.

PHILIP: (*To MILLER: surprised*) I didn't know you actually knew Teckman?

MILLER: Yes, we were in the R.A.F. together; we were never close friends of course, but –

HILTON: (*Interrupting*) What Squadron were you in, Mr Miller?

MILLER: (*Facing HILTON; puzzled by the question*) I beg your pardon?

HILTON: I said – what Squadron were you in?

MILLER: Why – the 16th …

PHILIP, obviously surprised, looks across at HILTON who is half smiling.

CUT TO: A corner table in a fashionable West End restaurant. *RICE is sitting at the table waiting for PHILIP; he is glancing through the pages of a magazine. A WAITER arrives and puts a glass of sherry down on the table.*

RICE: Thank you. (*He looks at his watch*)

WAITER: Would you like me to take your order, sir?

RICE: No, I'll give my friend another five minutes and then … (*Suddenly*) Ah, here we are!

PHILIP arrives; RICE rises and shakes hands. The WAITER stands near the table.

PHILIP: (*A shade breathless*) I'm most terribly sorry I'm late. I do apologise.

RICE: (*Pleasantly*) That's okay, think nothing of it. I'll bet you can use a drink right now.

PHILIP: I most certainly can!

PHILIP sits at the table.

WAITER: (*To PHILIP*) What can I get you, sir?

PHILIP: I'd like a pink gin.

WAITER: Certainly, sir.

The WAITER goes.

PHILIP: I thought I was never going to get here! The traffic in Oxford Street ...

RICE: (*Laughing*) I know – it gets worse every day. I'm afraid you'll find Berlin almost as bad. (*Smiling*) Well – are you looking forward to your trip?

PHILIP: (*Taking out his cigarette case and offering RICE a cigarette*) Yes, I am, but – I've had rather a worrying time since I saw you last.

RICE: Yes, so I gather. I saw a report in one of the newspapers.

PHILIP: Oh, you read about Garvin?

RICE: Yes. Was he a friend of yours?

PHILIP: No, I hardly knew him, except that I'd interviewed him the day before because he was a friend of Martin Teckman's and I'd been asked to write a book about him.

RICE: About Garvin?

PHILIP: No, no, Teckman.

RICE: Oh, yes of course, I remember your telling me. Tell me: have the police any idea who murdered Garvin?

PHILIP: I don't think so; if they have, they certainly haven't confided in me. I'm seeing the Inspector again this afternoon.

RICE: I see. Well, I hope this business isn't going to make any difference to our arrangements.

PHILIP: I don't see why it should; if they want me, I can always fly back.

44

RICE: Yes, of course. (*He takes two envelopes out of his pocket*) Well, here's your ticket and … Now where did I put that cheque? Oh, here we are! Mustn't forget the cheque, that's most important.

PHILIP: Thank you.

RICE: I've attached the Bank's letter for your convenience. It's made out for a thousand. I think that's what we agreed.

PHILIP: Yes.

RICE: The rest of the money will be paid into your account in London, except for your expenses of course, you'll draw those in Berlin. However, Kesner will give you all the details.

PHILIP: Kesner?

RICE: Yes, Rudolf Kesner – he's our Berlin representative. You'll like him, he's a great guy. I phoned him this morning and he said he'd do his best to meet the plane. If he doesn't meet it, go straight to the office. (*He hands PHILIP the envelopes*) There's a letter of introduction inside.

PHILIP: Thank you. And what about Hotel accommodation, shall I …

RICE: Kesner's already fixed it. Don't worry, he'll look after you. Oh, here's your ticket. (*He hands PHILIP the second envelope*)

PHILIP: (*After taking the ticket out of the envelope and looking at it*) Eleven fifteen …

RICE: Yeah – you should be in Berlin about four o'clock …

PHILIP: (*Pleased*) Jolly good!

WAITER: Would you like some water, sir?

PHILIP: Yes – that's enough.

RICE: I always spend the white one first – they make my wallet so bulky. Well – here's to a successful trip!

CUT TO: The drawing room of PHILIP's flat.

PHILIP is on the telephone.

PHILIP: Hello? … Is that the Central Bank? … Put me through to the Manager, will you please? … Oh, my name is Philip Chance … I've just received a cheque for a thousand pounds from a Mr John Rice … Yes, I understand he's got an account at your branch … Exactly, that's very good of you. I'd be awfully grateful if you would … Yes, I'll be in all afternoon … Sloane 1134 … Thank you.

PHILIP replaces the receiver as the doorbell rings. He goes to open the door and finds INSPECTOR HILTON outside.

HILTON: Good afternoon, sir!

PHILIP: Oh, hello, Inspector! Come in.

HILTON: Thank you.

HILTON comes in and the two men go through to the drawing room.

PHILIP: Well, any developments, Inspector?

HILTON: (*Looking round the flat*) Yes, one or two, sir. Nothing very startling, but – Oh, before I forget, Mr Chance. A Major Harris may be telephoning you …

PHILIP: Major Harris?

HILTON: Yes. He'd like to have a word with you.

PHILIP: Well – who is he?

HILTON: He's interested in the Garvin murder.

PHILIP: Yes, but – is he one of your people – is he attached to Scotland Yard?

HILTON: Er – yes, sir.   (*Takes a tiny notebook out of his pocket*) Mr Chance, I wonder if you would be good enough to confirm what you told me yesterday. It's the time element I'm interested in.

PHILIP: Well?

HILTON: (*Looking at the notebook*) I understand that after you left here yesterday morning you went shopping and arrived at your Club at about … (*Deliberately hesitates*)

PHILIP: About half past twelve.

HILTON: (*Nodding*) You had an appointment with a Mr Rice.

PHILIP: That's right.

HILTON: You left the Club at approximately …

PHILIP: Approximately three o'clock.

HILTON: So, we can safely say that you were at The Storey Club, from approximately twelve-thirty until … about three.

PHILIP: Yes.

HILTON: (*Replacing the notebook*) Thank you.

PHILIP: (*Quietly*) When was he murdered, Inspector?

HILTON: Well, of course, we can't be absolutely certain, but –

PHILIP: You're pretty certain.

HILTON: (*Nodding*) Yes.

PHILIP: Well?

A pause.

HILTON: (*Suddenly*) Not before one o'clock and no later than a quarter past two.

PHILIP: Thank goodness for that!

HILTON: (*Smiling*) Yes, a most convenient time, Mr Chance.

PHILIP: Was the murder committed here, do you think, or – ?

HILTON: No, he was brought here.

PHILIP: Are you sure?

HILTON: (*Quietly*) Yes, we're sure.

PHILIP: Then whoever brought him had a key?

HILTON: It looks very much like it. (*Nodding*) Well, thank you, sir. (*Crosses towards the alcove*) Oh, by the way – if I were you, I'd change my front door lock.

PHILIP: Yes, that's a very good idea. I'll try and get it done before I leave.

HILTON: (*Pleasantly*) Oh, of course! You're leaving for Berlin tomorrow, I was forgetting.

PHILIP: Yes. If you want an address where you can get in touch with me …

HILTON: (*Offhand; but with charm*) No, no, that's quite all right, Mr Chance.

The telephone starts ringing.

HILTON: (*Smiling*) We can always get you if we want you, sir.

PHILIP isn't quite sure how to take this.

PHILIP: (*Moving towards the telephone*) Will you excuse me?

HILTON: (*Nodding*) I'll let myself out. Have a good trip. Goodbye, sir!

HILTON goes out. PHILIP picks up the telephone receiver, although he still looks towards the alcove.

PHILIP: (*On phone*) Hello? … Oh, hello … Yes … Well, I thought the cheque would be all right but I just wanted to make certain … Yes, of course … It's most kind of you … Thank you for ringing … Goodbye.

PHILIP replaces the telephone receiver and then picks up the cheque and looks at it.

CUT TO: The Front Door of PHILIP's flat.

HELEN TECKMAN is pressing the doorbell. She waits a few moments then presses it again. After a pause PHILIP opens the door.

PHILIP: (*Surprised*) Why, hello! This is a surprise!

48

HELEN:	Do you remember me?
PHILIP:	Of course I remember you, Miss Teckman! Come in!

HELEN enters and the door is closed.

CUT TO: The Drawing Room of PHILIP's flat.
PHILIP and HELEN enter from the hall.

PHILIP:	Do sit down.
HELEN:	I hope I haven't called at a difficult time …
PHILIP:	No, of course not. I'm delighted to see you. As a matter of fact I nearly telephoned you the other day …
HELEN:	(*Smiling*) But you changed your mind?
PHILIP:	Yes, I did.
HELEN:	Why?
PHILIP:	Well, oddly enough after I met you my publisher asked me to write a book about your brother – Martin – that was when I nearly telephoned you – and then … (*He hesitates*)
HELEN:	Yes?
PHILIP:	(*Lamely*) Then I'm afraid I decided not to write the book. I received a better offer.

HELEN nods.

HELEN:	I see.
PHILIP:	(*After a moment*) I suppose you read about Garvin?
HELEN:	Yes, I did. That's why I came to see you. (*She takes a letter from her handbag*) I had a letter from him this morning and …
PHILIP:	From Garvin?
HELEN:	Yes, he must have posted it just before he was killed. He told me that he'd seen you and that you were going to write a book about my brother Martin.

49

PHILIP: (*Faintly embarrassed*) Oh, I see.

HELEN: Would you like to read the letter?

PHILIP: Well –

HELEN: I think, in view of what's happened, it might be very important.

PHILIP: Important?

HELEN: He says … 'I was most impressed by Chance; we got on awfully well together and I think he'll make a very good job of the biography. I hope you'll give him all the help you can, Helen.'

PHILIP: That's very kind of Garvin, but – forgive me – I don't quite see why you consider it important.

HELEN: Well, this letter proves that he liked you and that you got on well together, if the police suspect that …

PHILIP: You didn't think I'd murdered Garvin, did you?

HELEN: If I'd thought that I shouldn't have brought the letter.

PHILIP: No, of course not. That was a very nice gesture and I appreciate it. But the police think I'm a good boy now. I've got an alibi.

HELEN: I'm glad to hear that. I wonder if you'll forgive me if I ask you a very frank question?

PHILIP: Go on.

HELEN: Supposing you hadn't received another offer, would you still want to write the book?

PHILIP: Since we're being so frank – no.

HELEN: Because of what happened to Andrew Garvin?

PHILIP: Partly.

HELEN: But you surely don't think that Garvin was murdered because you went to see him?

PHILIP: I don't know why Garvin was murdered, but he was murdered, and he was murdered twenty-four hours after I saw him.

HELEN: I see.

PHILIP: (*Quietly*) Miss Teckman …

HELEN: Yes?

PHILIP: Did you like Andrew Garvin?

HELEN: (*After a slight hesitation*) No, not very much. He was far too eccentric and he drank too much.

PHILIP: Yes, I can imagine that.

HELEN: Did he show you the model that Martin made?

PHILIP: Of the B.109?

HELEN: Yes.

PHILIP: (*Nodding; watching her*) Yes, he showed it to me.

HELEN: Andrew had a theory about the B.109. He thought that the plane didn't disintegrate but landed somewhere …

PHILIP: Yes, I know – he told me.

HELEN: (*Smiling*) He would: he told nearly everybody. That's why he lost his job at Walters, because he just couldn't stop talking about it.

PHILIP: Miss Teckman – look I'm tired of calling you Miss Teckman – Helen – a few moments ago you asked me a very frank question. Now – do you mind if I ask you one?

HELEN: No.

PHILIP: What sort of a man was your brother?

HELEN: He was kind and generous, impetuous over some things, strangely tolerant over others. I remember a funny old don at Oxford saying 'Martin Teckman is the most unexceptional person I've ever met'.

51

PHILIP:	What could he have meant by that?
HELEN:	He meant that when you first met Martin you thought you were meeting just an ordinary, rather clever young undergraduate – then suddenly you realised that the young man in the grey flannel trousers and the blazer ...
PHILIP:	Was quite exceptional.
HELEN:	Yes.
PHILIP:	Miss Teckman, tell me; would you have described your brother in any way as a fanatic?
HELEN:	Good gracious, no! Why do you ask?
PHILIP:	Because of something that Garvin said. I just forget what it was, but I remember wondering at the time ...
HELEN:	No, you could never have called Martin a fanatic. But there were times when he became obsessed with things. Dear Martin ... I remember when he was seventeen. He bought a gramophone record of 'Charmaine'; it's a very old dance tune, you remember it, don't you?
PHILIP:	Yes, of course I do. (*He hums the opening bars of Charmaine*)
HELEN:	That's it! Well, Martin became obsessed with that tune. He never stopped playing it. My poor father broke six records before Martin was cured.
PHILIP:	(*Laughing*) I remember feeling exactly the same about 'Red Sails in the Sunset'. Is your father still alive?
HELEN:	No, both my parents are dead – they died at the beginning of the war.
PHILIP:	Oh, I'm sorry. (*Suddenly: taking the letter of introduction out of his inside pocket*) Miss Teck

	– Helen, I'm leaving for Berlin tomorrow morning …
HELEN:	Oh!
PHILIP:	I shall be away for about six months. I'd like you to take my address just in case …
HELEN:	Yes?
PHILIP:	Well – in case you'd like to get in touch with me at any time.
HELEN:	Thank you.
PHILIP:	You can write to me care of a Mr Rudolph Kesner, 128A, Kurfurstendam, Berlin, 4.
HELEN:	(*After a moment: quietly*) Why are you going away?
PHILIP:	I'm going to write some articles for an American magazine.
HELEN:	I see. Is that the only reason?
PHILIP:	Yes.
HELEN:	What are you going to write the articles on?
PHILIP:	Berlin.
HELEN:	Oh, I see.
PHILIP:	After I've been to Berlin, they may send me down to the South of France.
HELEN:	That should be nice for you.
PHILIP:	I'm very fond of the South of France. (*A pause*) Aren't you going to make a note of this address?
HELEN:	Mr Chance, why was Garvin murdered?
PHILIP:	I don't know.
HELEN:	Was it because of something he knew?
PHILIP:	Something he knew?
HELEN:	About the B.109?
PHILIP:	I just don't know.

CUT TO: *A shot of PHILIP arriving at London Airport by private car; he gets out of the car; takes two suitcases and a brief case from the back seat. Porters arrive from the Continental Departure Office and start to take possession of his luggage. PHILIP pays the driver of his car and the driver salutes him and turns the car round. As the car drives away it passes another car drawn up by the side of the drive. The driver of this car has been watching PHILIP's arrival. It is JOHN RICE.*

CUT TO: The Drawing Room of HELEN TECKMAN's Flat in Lowndes Square. It is tastefully furnished with obvious feminine touches.

DETECTIVE-INSPECTOR HILTON and MAJOR HARRIS are waiting for HELEN TECKMAN to appear. MAJOR HARRIS is a tall, rather suave individual. His manner is cold and quiet. PAT, a maid, appears from one of the other rooms.

PAT:　　Miss Teckman will be with you in a moment, sir.

HILTON: Thank you.

The maid goes out. HILTON notices a photograph on a small table; there is a telephone also on the table. He crosses and picks up the photograph.

HILTON: This is Teckman, isn't it?

HARRIS: (*Looking at the photograph*) Yes.

HILTON: Did you ever meet him?

HARRIS: Once.

HILTON: I'm – well, he doesn't look a very remarkable young man.

HARRIS: I can assure you he was.

HILTON: This must have been taken before the War. Funny how plus-fours went out of fashion, isn't it?

HELEN enters.

HELEN:　Good morning.

HILTON: (*Putting down the photograph; with charm*) Good morning, Miss Teckman. This is a colleague of mine, Major Harris.

HELEN: How do you do. Won't you sit down?

HELEN looks at HARRIS but neither of them speak.

HELEN: (*To HILTON*) Well – what can I do for you, Inspector?

HILTON: Well, now – I daresay you've guessed why we've come to see you. It's about Andrew Garvin. I understand he was a friend of your brother's.

HELEN: Yes, he was.

HILTON: A close friend?

HELEN: I suppose you'd call them close friends: they certainly saw a great deal of each other, particularly during the War.

HILTON: Ah, yes, of course. And after the War?

HELEN: They were at Walters-Armitage together, working on the B.109.

HILTON nods.

HARRIS: When did you see Garvin last, Miss Teckman?

HELEN: About a year ago, although curiously enough I had a letter from him the day before he was found murdered.

HARRIS: (*Curious*) Indeed?

HELEN: (*Frankly*) Would you like to see it?

HARRIS: (*Smiling*) Well, we'd certainly like to know what was in it.

HELEN: He was rather excited over the fact that he'd been interviewed by a writer called Philip Chance, who had told him that he intended writing a book about my brother.

HARRIS: Why should the prospect of a book about your brother excite Mr Garvin?

HELEN: I can't imagine – perhaps he thought he was going to be mentioned in it.

HARRIS: Miss Teckman, forgive me if I ask a rather personal question.

HELEN: I'm quite sure you're very experienced at asking personal questions, Major.

HARRIS: Were you on very friendly terms with your brother?

HELEN: Yes.

HARRIS: You saw a great deal of him?

HELEN: Not a great deal, but we were very good friends.

HARRIS: (*Taking out his wallet*) I have here a photograph of your brother. It was taken while he was at Walters-Armitage. (*He takes a snapshot out of his wallet*) There's another man in the picture, apparently a friend of your brother's. I wonder if you could identify him.

HELEN looks at the snapshot. HARRIS and the INSPECTOR watch her reaction.

HELEN: No, I've never seen him before. (*She returns the photograph to HARRIS*) But that's not surprising, my brother had a great many friends I knew nothing about.

HARRIS: You're quite sure you've never seen this man before?

HELEN: Quite sure.

HARRIS looks at the photograph.

HARRIS: (*Casually; almost without thinking*) The name Kesner doesn't mean anything to you, by any chance? Rudolph Kesner?

HELEN: (*Surprised*) Rudolph Kesner?

HARRIS: (*Looking up*) Yes …

HELEN: Why, yes, of course it does! Mr Chance has got a
         letter of introduction to a man called Rudolph
         Kesner.
HARRIS: (*Quickly, to HILTON*) What time does Chance
         leave?
HILTON: Eleven-fifteen, London Airport.
HARRIS grabs the telephone and starts to dial.

CUT TO: A B.E.A. Elizabethan Aircraft is on the runway at
London Airport: it is ready for the flight to Berlin. Luggage is
being loaded on to a tender ready to be taken out to the plane.
*JOAN (a B.E.A. uniformed airhostess) is standing in the
doorway of the Passenger Departure Building: she is watching
the plane; holding a passenger list in her hand. Passengers are
grouped behind her in the building.*

CUT TO: The interior of the building.
JOAN: Are your passengers ready?
BETTY: Yes, and not a film star in the lot. Have you got a
         Mr Philip Chance on the Berlin flight?
*JOAN looks at her list: actually, PHILIP has overheard the
remark and turns towards BETTY.*
JOAN: (*Looking at her list*) Yes …
PHILIP: I'm Philip Chance …
BETTY: Oh, will you come this way, please?
PHILIP: (*Puzzled*) Why? What is it?
BETTY walks away from PHILIP.
BETTY: This way, sir – please.
PHILIP follows her.

CUT TO: A small ante-room at London Airport.
*DETECTIVE-INSPECTOR HILTON, HELEN TECKMAN and
MAJOR HARRIS are present. The door is opened, and BETTY*

and PHILIP enter the room. PHILIP stops dead when he sees
HELEN and the INSPECTOR. BETTY closes the door.

PHILIP: (*Astonished*) Inspector! What's all this about?

HELEN: (*To PHILIP*) I don't know.

HARRIS: We saw Miss Teckman this morning and she told us that you had received …

PHILIP: (*Angry; looking at HARRIS*) What do you mean 'we'? Who's 'we'?

HARRIS: My name is Harris – Major Harris. I believe Inspector Hilton has already mentioned my name to you.

PHILIP: Oh, yes, that's right. He said that you were going to telephone me.

HARRIS: Unfortunately, I didn't.

PHILIP: Well, look here my plane's due to leave in five minutes, if you've got any questions to ask, for goodness sake be quick!

HARRIS: I understand that you are going to Berlin to write a series of magazine articles.

PHILIP: (*Impatient*) Yes, that's true. (*To HILTON*) You knew that, Inspector – I told you.

HILTON: Yes, sir. But you didn't tell me the name of the magazine.

PHILIP: Good heavens above, you don't mean to tell me that you've rushed me down here just to ask me the name of the magazine.

HARRIS: We didn't rush you here, Mr Chance, and we didn't come just to ask one pertinent question: however, since we are here, perhaps you'll enlighten us. What is the name of the magazine?

PHILIP: It's called "The New World".

HARRIS: "The New World"?

PHILIP: Yes.

HARRIS: And the name of the editor?

PHILIP: I don't know. I've never met the editor.

HARRIS: Indeed?

PHILIP: I've dealt with the European Representative: a man called John Rice.

HARRIS: Have you ever seen a copy of this – "New World"?

PHILIP: (*Resenting HARRIS's tone*) No, I haven't. But I have seen a cheque for a thousand pounds.

HARRIS: (*Intrigued*) Mr Rice gave you a cheque for a thousand pounds?

PHILIP: He did.

HARRIS: When?

PHILIP: When he gave me the ticket for Berlin.

HARRIS: And the cheque was perfectly all right?

PHILIP: Would I be flying to Berlin, if it wasn't?

HARRIS: What sort of a man is this Mr Rice?

PHILIP: He's an American; middle-aged; stout; going grey.

HILTON: Are you sure he's an American?

PHILIP: Well, he talks with an American accent.

HILTON: I see.

HARRIS takes the photograph he showed HELEN out of his pocket and holds it up so that PHILIP can see it.

HARRIS: Would that be your Mr Rice by any chance?

PHILIP: (*Looking at the photograph*) Good heavens, no! He's much older than that, besides … (*Suddenly*) but wait a minute! (*Takes the photograph from HARRIS and stares at it*) This other man … (*To HELEN*) … Isn't that your brother?

HELEN: Yes.

HILTON: (*Nodding*) That's Martin Teckman all right, but it's the other gentleman we're interested in.

PHILIP: Well, it's not Rice.

HARRIS: (*Taking the photograph back*) No, I didn't think it was. As a matter of fact, we know who it is …

59

PHILIP: If you'll just tell me the rules, I'll play the game with you.

HARRIS: It's a man called Kesner – Rudolph Kesner.

PHILIP: (*Astonished*) Rudolph Kesner?

HARRIS: Yes.

PHILIP: But I've got a letter of introduction to a man called Rudolph Kesner. I'm supposed to be meeting him in Berlin.

HARRIS: So I understand.

PHILIP looks at HELEN, then at the INSPECTOR, and finally at HARRIS. Suddenly he takes the letter out of his pocket, and rips open the envelope. He takes a single quarto sheet of notepaper out of the envelope, but before he can unfold it HARRIS reaches out and takes it out of his hand. PHILIP retains the envelope.

HARRIS: If you please …

HARRIS slowly unfolds the piece of notepaper; he stares at it for a little while and then looks up.

HARRIS: Would you like to see your letter of introduction, Mr Chance?

He holds out the piece of notepaper. On it is a drawing of the B.109.

CUT TO: The Drawing Room of HELEN TECKMAN's Flat.

HELEN: I shouldn't worry, Philip, if I were you.

PHILIP: But I can't help worrying. Why do you think I accepted Rice's offer in the first place? Because I wanted to get away from this business. Because I didn't want to get involved in the Teckman affair. If Rice is mixed up in it, and he obviously is, I'm in a worse mess than ever.

HELEN: Yes, but you can prove that it was a business proposition. Rice gave you a cheque.

PHILIP: Yes, thank goodness! (*Looking at his watch*) Half-past nine. If I'd caught that plane, I'd have been in Berlin five hours ago.

HELEN: Yes.

PHILIP: I wonder what would have happened? Do you think I'd have seen Kesner?

HELEN: Yes, I do, because I think that letter was important. It's my bet Kesner would have met you at the airport.

PHILIP: Well, if the letter was so important, why didn't Rice give it to someone he knew?

HELEN: He did. He gave it to you – and he knew that he could trust you because you hadn't the slightest idea what was in the letter.

PHILIP: Yes, I suppose that's true. Did you see it?

HELEN: Yes. It was a drawing of the B.109.

PHILIP: All that talk about a series of magazine articles was obviously just eyewash.

HELEN: Except that he did pay you a thousand pounds.

PHILIP: Yes, and now I know why!

HELEN: Why?

PHILIP: Because he wanted me out of the way: he didn't want me to write the Teckman biography.

HELEN: Well, why should Rice or anyone else try to stop you from writing a book about my brother? After all, I'm the only person who could really object …

PHILIP: (*A shade surprised by the thought*) Yes, if it comes to that, I suppose you are.

HELEN: (*After a moment; hesitant*) Philip …

PHILIP: Yes?

HELEN: I'm sorry about this morning.

PHILIP: What do you mean?

HELEN: Well, if I hadn't told Major Harris that you'd mentioned the name Kesner, he would never have jumped to the conclusion that ...

PHILIP: My dear young lady, I'm delighted you told Harris! If you hadn't have done so, I'd have caught the plane and then heaven only knows what might have happened to me!

HELEN smiles and PHILIP notices that she is amused.

PHILIP: You can smile, but this isn't my idea of fun and games!

HELEN: I didn't think it was. Strictly the South of France type.

PHILIP: That's me.

HELEN: No responsibility at any price.

PHILIP: None.

HELEN: Are you really as irresponsible as you make yourself out to be?

PHILIP: Oh, absolutely – it isn't an act.

HELEN: Well, I'm not really convinced. I'm quite sure you're the strong silent type.

PHILIP: (*Shaking his head*) You're thinking of Gregory Peck. Believe me, I'm the last person to get mixed up in this sort of thing. "Take no Chances, Chance" – that's the family motto – always has been.

HELEN laughs. The telephone rings.

HELEN: (*Turning towards the telephone*) Excuse me. (*She lifts the receiver*) Hello?

MAN's VOICE: (*On the other end of the line*) Is that Sloane 9846?

HELEN: Yes ...

MAN's VOICE: Can I speak to Miss Teckman, please?

HELEN: (*Puzzled*) This is Miss Teckman speaking ...

CUT TO: The MAN in a telephone box. It is the MAN in episode one whose overcoat was mislaid.

MAN: Is that you, Helen?

HELEN: (*Still very puzzled*) Yes …

MAN: Well – how are you after all this time?

CUT back to HELEN. She is obviously very puzzled.

HELEN: Who is that? Who is it speaking?

CUT back to the MAN in the telephone box.

MAN: Don't you know, Helen? Don't you know?

The MAN smiles; moves nearer to the mouthpiece, and commences to whistle "Charmaine".

END OF EPISODE TWO

EPISODE THREE

47 HARRISON COURT

OPEN TO: *A MAN is standing in a telephone box talking on the phone*.

MAN: Is that you, Helen?

HELEN: (*On the other end of the line: still very puzzled*) Yes …

MAN: Well – how are you after all this time?

CUT back to *HELEN in her drawing room. PHILIP is in the near background. HELEN is obviously very puzzled*.

HELEN: Who is that? Who is it speaking?

CUT back to the MAN in the telephone box.

MAN: Don't you know, Helen? Don't you know?

The MAN smiles; moves nearer to the mouthpiece, and commences to whistle "Charmaine".

CUT back to HELEN. She is speechless; aghast.

PHILIP: What is it? (*He moves nearer to HELEN*) Helen, what's the matter?

HELEN: (*Softly; bewildered*) It's – It's Martin.

PHILIP: Martin? You mean your brother? Why, that's impossible, he … (*Suddenly*) Give me the phone! (*Quickly takes the receiver from HELEN*) Hello? Hello, who is that?

CUT back to the MAN in the telephone box: on hearing PHILIP's voice he replaces the receiver.

CUT back to PHILIP.

PHILIP: (*On the phone*) Hello? … Hello? (*Taps the receiver*) Hello … (*He replaces the receiver*)

HELEN: (*Tensely; overwrought*) It was Martin! I'm sure it was Martin … Philip, what does this mean? If he's alive then why doesn't he …

PHILIP: (*Quietly; taking her by the arm*) Now wait a minute! Wait a minute, Helen! (*A moment; softly*) Now what happened exactly?

HELEN: (*Trying to gain control of herself*) When I asked who it was speaking, he said … "*Don't you know, Helen? Don't you know?*" … Then he …

PHILIP: (*Interrupting*) But that doesn't prove anything, unless you recognised his voice …

HELEN: … Then he whistled "Charmaine".

PHILIP: "Charmaine"?

HELEN: (*Quickly*) Don't you remember? I told you, that was a favourite tune of Martin's.

PHILIP: You're sure he whistled "Charmaine"? It wasn't just your imagination?

HELEN: No, no … It was Martin! I know it was Martin! (*Tensely*) Don't you see, Garvin was right! The B.109 didn't crash, and if it didn't crash then obviously … (*Suddenly, picking up the telephone receiver*) We've got to tell the police!

PHILIP: (*Interrupting*) Wait a minute.

PHILIP puts his hand on HELEN's and stops her from dialling.

PHILIP: Now, assuming for the moment, that it was your brother, doesn't it strike you as being a little odd that he hasn't already contacted the police – or at any rate contacted you, or the people he worked for?

HELEN: Perhaps he's ill; perhaps he's suffering from amnesia. You do hear of cases like that …

PHILIP: Yes, but this isn't one of them.

HELEN: What do you mean?

PHILIP: Now listen, Helen. If he didn't know who he was then he wouldn't have remembered you, in which case how could he have telephoned you?

HELEN: Yes, that's true, but if he's perfectly all right why hasn't he been in touch with me before? It's over eighteen months since the B.109 crashed.

PHILIP: There's two possible explanations. One: that wasn't your brother on the phone but somebody playing a diabolical trick on you …

HELEN: (*Shocked*) But who would do a thing like that?

PHILIP: Or it was your brother and for some unknown reason he's been lying low and daren't report to the authorities or even get in touch with you.

HELEN: I think that's the most likely explanation.

PHILIP: Then why did he telephone tonight? And having telephoned why didn't he tell you, quite simply, who he was?

HELEN: (*Tensely*) I don't know …

PHILIP: (*A moment; thoughtfully*) Well, if it was your brother it looks as if that theory of Garvin's wasn't so ridiculous after all.

HELEN: Yes, and yet …

PHILIP: Well?

HELEN: (*Suddenly*) Philip, supposing it was Martin …

PHILIP: Yes?

HELEN: Do you think the fact that he's alive has got anything to do with … (*Hesitates*)

PHILIP: With what?

HELEN: With why Barbara Jefferies was knocked down by that car, with why you were sent to Berlin?

PHILIP: Yes. (*Nodding*) You can't write a biography without delving into the past of the person you're writing about. Someone – possibly Rice – didn't want either Barbara or me to make too many inquiries about Martin Teckman.

HELEN: But Rice gave you a cheque for a thousand pounds. That's an awful lot of money just to stop someone from writing a biography.

PHILIP: (*Nodding*) I've been thinking about that cheque. Have you got a London Telephone Directory, Helen … A. to D.?

HELEN: Yes. (*She crosses to the bureau and takes a directory out of a drawer*) What do you want it for?

PHILIP: Rice gave me a piece of paper with the name of his bank and the telephone number on it. He said he was moving his flat and if I wanted to get in touch with him the best thing I could do was to write to the bank. Like a fool, that was the number I phoned when I enquired about the cheque.

HELEN: (*Turning the pages of the directory*) What was the name of the bank?

PHILIP: The Central, Throgmorton Street. (*He takes a piece of paper out of his inside pocket*)

HELEN: (*Looking up from the directory*) The Central Bank, 287, Throgmorton Street, E.C.4. …

PHILIP: That's it.

HELEN: What's your number?

PHILIP: (*Looking at his piece of paper*) City 9873 …

HELEN: No … Mansion House 9632 …

PHILIP: Mr Rice seems to have thought of everything. (*Suddenly; putting the piece of paper back in his pocket*) Helen, look – it's no good discussing this business any more tonight. We've had a pretty hectic day and we're tired. I suggest you call round and see me tomorrow morning, we'll have another talk about the phone call and if you still

70

	feel you want to tell the police about it, I'll ring the Inspector myself.
HELEN:	Yes, all right. (*Softly*) You're very kind.
PHILIP:	(*Looking at HELEN*) That call gave you a pretty nasty shock, didn't it?

HELEN nods.

PHILIP:	Well, if you're nervous during the night or get worried about anything, just give me a tinkle. I'll be round like a shot.
HELEN:	(*Smiling*) Yes, all right.
PHILIP:	Why are you smiling?
HELEN:	I was just thinking of that family motto of yours. "Take no chances ..."
PHILIP:	Oh, don't worry about that. I was the black sheep of the family anyway.

CUT TO: The Front Door of PHILIP's flat.

PHILIP arrives carrying his suitcase and briefcase; he takes out his key and lets himself into the flat.

CUT TO: The Drawing Room of PHILIP's flat.

PHILIP enters. He switches on the table lamp, then puts down his suitcase and briefcase and takes off his hat and coat.

RICE:	(*Out of shot*) Good evening!

PHILIP turns quickly and sees RICE sitting in an armchair watching him.

PHILIP:	(*Tensely*) What are you doing here? How did you get into the flat?
RICE:	(*Rising*) I'll give you three guesses. (*Smiling*) I used a key.

PHILIP moves across to the telephone and picks up the receiver.

RICE:	(*With authority*) Don't touch that phone!

PHILIP hesitates, then slowly replaces the receiver.

71

PHILIP: Now look here, Rice, I don't know what the game is …

RICE: You're not supposed to know what the game is; you're just supposed to do as you're told.

PHILIP: Really? This is a new approach, isn't it, Mr Rice?

RICE: What happened at the Airport? Why didn't you catch the plane?

PHILIP: I suddenly felt rather homesick. I thought of my flat, Regents Park, the lights in Piccadilly …

RICE: (*Controlling his anger*) Mr Chance, I'm asking you why you didn't catch that plane?

PHILIP: (*Facing him; quite calmly*) And I'm telling you. I felt homesick. Nostalgic. You know the feeling; a sensitive person like yourself, you must have felt it a hundred times.

RICE: (*A moment; quietly*) Why didn't you catch that plane?

PHILIP: (*Suddenly; smiling*) But I did catch it, didn't you know? I arrived in Berlin at precisely four forty-five. I was met by a Mr Kesner who treated me like a brother – or should I say comrade?

RICE: You must forgive me if I don't appreciate your sense of humour, but unfortunately …

PHILIP: That's all right, old boy. You'll get used to it. It's an acquired taste.

RICE: Not for me it isn't. (*He takes a revolver out of his pocket*) I'm going to ask you the question once more. If you don't answer it …

PHILIP: (*Suddenly; almost losing his temper*) I didn't catch the plane because I wasn't allowed to catch it!

RICE: Why?

PHILIP: Don't you know why?

RICE: You mean – the police changed their mind. They wouldn't let you go?

72

PHILIP: Yes.

RICE: What happened?

PHILIP: Well, they just didn't believe me. They didn't believe that I was going to Berlin to write magazine articles. As a matter of fact, I began to doubt it myself.

RICE: Did you tell them about Kesner?

PHILIP: Of course. They were most interested. They showed me a photograph of him ...

RICE: (*Surprised*) Of Kesner?

PHILIP: Yes, of Kesner. Rudolph Kesner, himself. In person.

RICE: (*Quickly*) When was the photograph taken?

PHILIP: (*A moment*) I don't know.

RICE: Was it a recent one?

PHILIP: I don't know.

RICE: (*Threatening*) I warn you, Mr Chance. (*A moment*) Was it a photograph of Kesner with a man called Martin Teckman?

PHILIP: Oh, so Mr Kesner is a friend of Martin Teckman's is he? Now that's interesting. When I mentioned Teckman to you the other day you pretended ...

RICE: (*Angry*) Answer my question! Was it a photograph of Kesner with Martin Teckman?

PHILIP: (*Losing his temper*) No, it wasn't! It was a photograph of Kesner on Brighton pier. He was sucking rock and stuffing himself with shrimps.

RICE: Mr Chance, I warn you for the last time, I don't like your sense of humour.

PHILIP: I'm not madly keen myself, old boy, but you know what a sense of humour is, you're stuck with it. However, if it's a laugh you want, I'll hand you a big one.

RICE: What do you mean?

PHILIP: I'm going to stick my neck out, Mr Rice. I'm going to probe. I'm going to investigate until I know everything there is to know about Teckman – and then I'm going to write. I'm going to write the book you, and your friends, don't want me to write – The Teckman Biography.

RICE: (*Slowly; watching PHILIP*) I hope you take your time over it, Mr Chance. It'll be your last book – if you ever write it. (*Suddenly*) And now – you have a letter I gave you, a letter of introduction.

PHILIP: Ah, I was wondering when we were coming to the letter.

RICE: The letter was intended for Kesner, but since you didn't …

The telephone starts ringing.

PHILIP: (*Interrupting*) The letter may have been intended for Kesner, but it never reached him.

RICE: I know that. That's why I want it back.

PHILIP: What makes you think I've still got it?

RICE: (*Anxiously*) Haven't you got it?

PHILIP: (*Smiling; turning towards the telephone*) You'd like to know, wouldn't you, Mr Rice?

PHILIP turns his back on RICE and picks up the telephone. RICE is angry; uncertain of himself, he suddenly makes a decision.

PHILIP: (*On phone*) Hello?

RUTH's Voice: (*On the other end*) Is that Sloane 1872?

PHILIP: Yes …

RICE clubs PHILIP on the back of the head with the handle of the revolver. PHILIP falls.

RUTH's Voice: (*On the phone*) Hello? … Can you hear me? … Hello? … Hello?

RICE picks up the receiver and replaces it; he then stoops down by PHILIP and commences to go through his pockets.

74

From the inside pocket he takes the envelope which contained the letter of introduction to Kesner. He turns the empty envelope over in his hand.

CUT TO: The Drawing Room of PHILIP's Flat.
It is some time later. RICE has departed. PHILIP is on the floor; semi-unconscious and gradually raises himself from the floor. He holds on to the small table. He stands, hands over his eyes, leaning against the table. The telephone starts to ring. PHILIP moves round the table, still obviously dazed and very uncertain of himself. He gropes and picks up the telephone.

RUTH's voice:*(On the other end)* Hello? ... Hello – is that Sloane 1872?

PHILIP: What – what's that?

RUTH's voice: I said, is that Sloane 1872?

PHILIP: Yes, I think so, I ...

CUT TO: RUTH WADE holding a telephone and sitting on the arm of a large armchair in a corner of her flat. There is a man in the armchair, but he is not visible, we can just see his hand, over the side of the chair, holding a cigar. He is obviously listening to the telephone conversation.

RUTH: *(On the phone: a shade angry)* Hello? Can you hear me?

PHILIP: *(On the other end: dazed)* Yes, I can hear you only I ... I ...

RUTH: I want to speak to Mr Philip Chance.

CUT Back to PHILIP.

PHILIP: *(Holding on to the table)* This is Chance speaking, you'll have to ...

RUTH: *(On the other end)* Hello ... I can't hear you, speak up please ...

PHILIP: (*His hand over his eyes; trying to gain control of himself*) I'm sorry … You'll have to ring tomorrow sometime, I – I can't talk now … (*He replaces the receiver*)

CUT Back to RUTH, who is replacing her receiver. She is obviously puzzled.

MAN: (*Out of picture*) What is it? What's the matter?

RUTH: I don't know. If that was Chance he was either drunk or ill or something. I couldn't get any sense out of him.

The camera tracks back and we now see that the man in the armchair is DAVID JEFFERIES.

JEFFERIES: Well; what did he say?

RUTH: He wants me to ring again tomorrow.

JEFFERIES: (*Nodding*) All right, you must ring tomorrow.

CUT TO: MAURICE MILLER's Office.

This is a small, compact office, with old fashioned, dignified fittings and furniture.

MILLER is sitting behind his desk writing a letter. He finishes a letter as HECTOR BRIGGS enters. BRIGGS is about thirty-five and is studious looking.

BRIGGS: Good morning, sir.

MILLER: (*Looking up*) Oh, hello, Briggs. I want you to get the Fairley contract and ask Miss Dawson to make three copies of it. Substitute the name Philip Chance, cut out the reference to Foreign rights and leave the title blank.

BRIGGS: Yes, sir. (*Curious*) Hasn't Mr Chance gone to Berlin, sir?

MILLER: No, I had a phone call from him about ten minutes ago.

BRIGGS: Well, this is a surprise, sir. What made him change his mind?

MILLER: Don't be silly, Hector – He's an author. Whatever makes an author change his mind.

BRIGGS: (*Smiling*) Well, there's one outside that won't change it. He insists on seeing you, sir.

MILLER: All right – send him in.

BRIGGS goes out and returns a few moments later with MAJOR HARRIS.

MILLER: Good morning, Mr –?

HARRIS: Harris.

BRIGGS goes out.

MILLER: Won't you sit down?

HARRIS nods and sits in the chair opposite the desk.

MILLER: Now, Mr Harris, what can I do for you?

HARRIS takes a small leather wallet out of his inside pocket and shows MILLER his card which is displayed inside the wallet.

MILLER: (*Surprised*) Oh, I beg your pardon, Major. I wouldn't have kept you waiting if I'd known, but they told me …

HARRIS: (*Replacing his wallet*) That's all right, sir. It was a new experience for me.

MILLER: Being kept waiting?

HARRIS: No, being mistaken for an author. Mr Miller, I understand that you propose publishing the biography of Martin Teckman?

MILLER: Yes.

HARRIS: Correct me if I'm mistaken, but before you approached Philip Chance didn't you ask Barbara Jefferies to write it?

MILER: Yes, I did.

HARRIS: Why?

MILLER: (*A shade surprised by the question*) Well – I thought she was the most suitable person. She's a very good writer and when I suggested the idea, she seemed very keen on it.

HARRIS: You suggested the idea to Mrs Jefferies, she didn't suggest it to you?

MILLER: That's right.

HARRIS: What made you think of the idea in the first place?

MILLER: (*A shrug*) There was a great deal in the newspapers about Teckman, everyone seemed interested in the B.109 – it seemed a very good idea to have a book written about him.

HARRIS: He wasn't a friend of yours by any chance?

MILLER: Teckman?

HARRIS: Yes.

MILLER: No; but we did know each other – we were in the RAF together.

HARRIS: (*Politely interested*) Oh, indeed?

MILLER: But I expect you knew that.

HARRIS: (*Ignoring the remark*) Mr Miller, tell me: did you ever meet any of Teckman's friends, any of his associates?

MILLER: No. (*Suddenly*) Oh, I met Andrew Garvin once. I went to Oxford for the day and Teckman introduced us. Garvin was lecturing at one of the Colleges.

HARRIS: I see. Were you surprised when you heard that Garvin had been murdered?

MILLER: Naturally. Is that why you're making these inquiries, because of the murder?

HARRIS: Partly – and partly because we're interested in Teckman.

MILLER: But Teckman's dead.

78

HARRIS: Mr Miller, when was the last time you saw Teckman?

MILLER: Oh, just before the War ended – February '45.

HARRIS: You haven't seen him since?

MILLER: No.

HARRIS: You're sure?

MILLER: Yes – quite sure.

A moment.

HARRIS: (*Pleasantly*) I understand you're very fond of Switzerland, Mr Miller.

MILLER: Yes, I go there nearly every year.

HARRIS: You went there in '47?

MILLER: Did I? I can't remember …

HARRIS: You stayed a week in Berne, four days in Kandersteg and ten days at Lausanne.

MILLER: Yes, I believe I did, now you come to mention it!

A moment.

HARRIS: (*Watching MILLER*) Didn't you have a drink with Martin Teckman in the Cornavin Hotel in Geneva?

MILLER: (*Suddenly; apparently genuinely surprised*) By George, yes! Of course I did! That's perfectly true. I was motoring through Geneva and I suddenly saw Teckman looking in a shop window. I pulled into the side and we went and had a drink together. (*Smiling at Harris*) Do you know, I'd completely forgotten all about it.

HARRIS: I thought you had, Mr Miller. (*Smiling at MILLER*) I thought you had.

CUT TO: The Drawing Room of PHILIP's flat.

MRS LACEY, PHILIP's housekeeper, is putting a small piece of Elastoplast on PHILIP's head. He is sitting on the arm of one of the armchairs; his jacket is over the back of one of the small chairs.

MRS LACEY: Does that feel comfy, sir?

PHILIP: Yes, that's fine, Mrs Lacey.

The doorbell rings.

MRS LACEY: I can't understand how it happened, sir. It's such a nasty little bump.

PHILIP: I've told you, I slipped while I was getting in the bath.

MRS LACEY: Well, you want to be more careful. Look well if you'd knocked yourself out. (*She crosses towards the alcove*)

PHILIP: If that's Miss Teckman ask her in.

MRS LACEY goes out. PHILIP takes his jacket off the chair and puts it on. MRS LACEY returns with HELEN.

MRS LACEY: Miss Teckman, sir.

PHILIP: Hello, Helen!

HELEN: Good morning! Am I too early for you?

PHILIP: No, of course not. Oh, by the way, this is my housekeeper Mrs Lacey – Miss Teckman.

HELEN: Good morning, Mrs Lacey.

MRS LACEY: How-do-you-do, Miss?

MRS LACEY goes out into the kitchen.

PHILIP: Well, how are you?

HELEN: I didn't have a very good night, I'm afraid.

PHILIP: No, I don't expect you did.

HELEN: I tried to get you on the phone this morning, but you were engaged.

PHILIP: Really – what time was that?

HELEN: About ten o'clock.

PHILIP: Yes, I had quite a long talk to Miller, my publisher. By the way, have you had breakfast?

HELEN: Yes, ages ago.

PHILIP: Would you like some coffee?

HELEN: No, thank you.

PHILIP: Well – any more telephone calls?

HELEN:	Yes …
PHILIP:	(*Surprised*) Really? You don't mean to say …
HELEN:	No, not like last night, but – Sir Charles Shaughnessy telephoned me.
PHILIP:	Sir Charles Shaughnessy? Isn't he the head of Walters-Armitage?
HELEN:	Yes.
PHILIP:	Well, what did he want?
HELEN:	He wants to see me: as a matter of fact, he's invited us to lunch.
PHILIP:	Us?
HELEN:	Yes. I asked him what he wanted to see me about, and he said it was something to do with my brother. I told him I had an appointment with you …
PHILIP:	(*Smiling*) And he invited me to lunch?
HELEN:	Not exactly. I told him you were going to write a book about Martin – that's why he invited you.
PHILIP:	Oh, I see. What sort of a man is Sir Charles Shaughnessy?
HELEN:	Well, I don't really know. I've only met him twice before.
PHILIP:	Were you surprised when he telephoned you?
HELEN:	Very. He sounded rather …
PHILIP:	Well?
HELEN:	Well, I thought he sounded rather agitated. I suppose it's difficult to judge when you don't really know a person.
PHILIP:	Yes.
HELEN:	(*A moment*) Philip, I've thought quite a lot about that phone call last night. I know you'll think I'm crazy, I know everyone will, but … I'm quite convinced that it was Martin.

PHILIP: (*Shaking his head*) I don't see how it could
               have been, Helen. I – just don't believe it's
               possible. (*A tiny pause*) You say, Shaughnessy
               said he wanted to see you because of something
               to do with Martin?
HELEN: Yes.
PHILIP: He didn't give you any idea of what it was?
HELEN: No.
(*A pause*)
HELEN: What are you thinking?
PHILIP: Nothing, I just …
HELEN: No, please!
PHILIP: It was nothing, Helen, I just had a sudden
               thought, that's all.
HELEN: Philip, please!
PHILIP: Well, I wondered if by any chance Sir Charles
               had received a telephone call.
HELEN: Yes, I wondered that.
PHILIP: Well, we'll soon find out. I'll get my things.

CUT TO: The outside of the house in Lowndes Square in
which PHILIP has his flat. PHILIP's car is parked outside.
PHILIP and HELEN come out of the house and get into the car.
PHILIP drives the car away. DAVID JEFFERIES is watching
the departure of the car from his own car which is parked on
the opposite side of the road. JEFFERIES gets out of his car
and crosses the door and enters the house.

CUT TO: The Front Door of PHILIP's flat.
DAVID JEFFERIES arrives in his outdoor clothes from the
street. He presses the door bell and the door is opened, after a
moment or two, by MRS LACEY.
JEFFERIES: Good morning! Could I see Mr Chance, please?
MRS LACEY: I'm sorry, sir, but Mr Chance is out.

82

JEFFERIES: Oh, dear! (*Pleasantly*) It's Mrs Lacey, isn't it?

MRS LACEY: That's right, sir.

JEFFERIES: I thought I recognised you. I'm David Jefferies, a friend of Mr Chance's.

MRS LACEY: Oh, yes, of course! How silly of me … Well, you've only just missed Mr Chance, sir – he left about three minutes ago.

JEFFERIES: Oh, what a pity! I wonder if he's gone to the Club? I don't suppose you happen to know …

MRS LACEY: I don't think so, sir. He had a young lady with him.

JEFFERIES: Oh. Miss –?

MRS LACEY: Teckman, sir. I believe they've gone out of Town for the day. I heard Mr Chance say something about a place called Walters … Walters something or other.

JEFFERIES: (*Surprised; interested*) Walters-Armitage?

MRS LACEY: Yes, that's it. Walters-Armitage. (*Curious*) Is it a village, sir?

JEFFERIES: (*His thoughts elsewhere*) No, not exactly, Mrs Lacey. Well – tell Mr Chance I called.

MRS LACEY: Yes, I will indeed, sir.

JEFFERIES: Goodbye.

MRS LACEY: Goodbye, sir.

MRS LACEY closes the door.

CUT TO: The Office of SIR CHARLES SHAUGHNESSY at Walters-Armitage Works.

This is a well-furnished office typical of a top rank industrialist. There are telephones, inter-office speakers etc on SIR CHARLES' desk.

SIR CHARLES, a rather distinguished looking man in his early sixties, is sitting behind his desk facing HELEN and PHILIP.

They have just finished coffee and SIR CHARLES is lighting a cigar.

SHAUGHNESSY: Who's going to publish this book of yours, Mr Chance?

PHILIP: Maurice Miller.

SHAUGHNESSY: (*Nodding*) A very good firm. Are you under contract to them?

PHILIP: For my novels, yes – but this is the first time I've attempted a biography.

SHAUGHNESSY: Well, any help we can give you – we shall be only too pleased.

PHILIP: Thank you.

SHAUGHNESSY: As a matter of fact, a thought just occurred to me. (*To HELEN*) Do you remember your brother reading a paper to our Science Club: it was when he first came here, just after the war?

HELEN: Yes, I believe I do.

SHAUGHNESSY: (*To PHILIP*) Awfully good paper. The Technical Press gave it a wonderful write-up.

PHILIP: Is it possible to read it?

SHAUGHNESSY: Yes, that's what I was going to suggest. We've got a copy on our file.

HELEN: (*To SHAUGHNESSY*) But wouldn't it be too technical for Mr Chance?

SHAUGHNESSY: I don't think so; there was an awful lot of personal stuff in it. Reminiscences about schooldays; University; that sort of thing.

PHILIP: It might be very useful.

SHAUGHNESSY: I think it would. (*He presses a switch on the inter-office speaker: into microphone*) I want you to bring me a copy of a paper written by Martin Teckman. It's on the T.

84

File under K.14, it's marked personal … (*Releasing the switch*) Your brother was a very remarkable young man, Miss Teckman. We've missed him at Walters. The great thing about Martin was that he was not only an enthusiast; he had vision, foresight. When he believed in a thing, he had the guts to say so.

PHILIP: Did he ever express any political opinions, Sir Charles?

SHAUGHNESSY: Good heavens, no! We never discuss politics here. We've got far too much to worry about without worrying about politics.

HELEN: (*Quietly*) Sir Charles …

SHAUGHNESSY: Yes, my dear?

HELEN: We've had a most enjoyable lunch and it's been nice seeing you again, but –

SHAUGHNESSY: Why did I send for you?

HELEN: Yes.

SIR CHARLES rises and walks round his desk.

SHAUGHNESSY: Yesterday morning a man called Major Harris came to see me. He asked me a great many questions about your brother, about the B.109 and about a man we used to have working for us called Andrew Garvin. Garvin was a clever old boy, but – well, a bit of a crank. He had a theory about the B.109 which we all knew about and which, quite frankly, we treated as a joke. Well, to cut a long story short, Harris knew all about Garvin's theory and he questioned me about it. I didn't attach a great deal of importance

	to this but last night, on my way home, a rather curious thing happened.
HELEN:	Go on, Sir Charles.
SHAUGHNESSY:	My car was turning out of the Strand when a man stepped off the pavement straight in front of it. Fortunately, my chauffeur braked, the man jumped back on the pavement and – disappeared into the crowd.

A pause.

SHAUGHNESSY:	(*To HELEN*) I hesitate to say what I'm now going to say because, quite obviously, you'll think it was my imagination. (*A moment*) That man was either Martin Teckman, or his double.

HELEN looks across at PHILIP. There is a pause.

HELEN:	(*Quietly*) Have you told anyone else about this?
SHAUGHNESSY:	No. No one. I wanted to tell you first because it occurred to me that if by any chance … (*Hesitates*) Well – if by any chance it was your brother …
HELEN:	I might have heard from him?
SHAUGHNESSY:	(*Nodding*) Yes.

There is another pause.

HELEN:	Martin was killed when the B.109 crashed. I've no reason to think otherwise, Sir Charles.
SHAUGHNESSY:	(*A moment, politely nodding*) Thank you, Miss Teckman – that's what I wanted to know. (*He looks up, towards the door*) Yes, what is it?
FEMALE voice:	(*Out of picture, from the doorway*) I've brought the paper you asked for, sir.
SHAUGHNESSY:	Ah, yes! Put it on the desk.

RUTH WADE is the female standing in the doorway, holding the manuscript.

CUT TO: The Drawing Room of PHILIP's flat.
MRS LACEY comes out of the kitchen carrying a tray of sandwiches and drinks. She places the tray on the small table, then goes back into the kitchen. PHILIP enters wearing his hat and coat. He is taking them off as MRS LACEY returns from the kitchen. She is now wearing her outdoor things.

PHILIP: Hello, Mrs Lacey! I thought you'd have left by now!

MRS LACEY: I've been making some sandwiches, sir.

PHILIP: Oh, it's very good of you, Mrs Lacey, but you shouldn't have bothered.

MRS LACEY: I thought Miss Teckman might be coming back with you, sir.

PHILIP: No, I dropped her at her flat. (*Putting down his coat*) Any messages?

MRS LACEY: Oh, a Mr Jefferies called …

PHILIP: Really? What time was that?

(*The door bell rings*)

MRS LACEY: Soon after you left, sir. I'm surprised you didn't bump into him.

PHILIP: Did he leave any message?

MRS LACEY: No, sir.

PHILIP: All right, Mrs Lacey. Oh, that's probably Mr Miller. If it is, ask him in.

MRS LACEY: Yes, sir.

MRS LACEY goes out. PHILIP picks up his hat and goes into the bedroom. MRS LACEY returns with MAURICE MILLER.

MRS LACEY: Mr Chance won't be a moment, sir.

MILLER: Thank you.

PHILIP re-enters.

MILLER: Hello, Philip!

PHILIP: My word, you're punctual – it's just seven o'clock.

MRS LACEY: Is there anything else, Mr Chance?

PHILIP: No, that's all right, thank you.

MRS LACEY: Goodnight, sir.

PHILIP: Goodbye, Mrs Lacey!

MILLER: (*To MRS LACEY*) Goodnight!

LACEY: Goodnight, sir!

MRS LACEY goes out.

MILLER: Philip, I can't tell you how delighted I was when you telephoned this morning.

PHILIP: I thought you'd be pleased.

MILLER: What made you change your mind? Did the Berlin thing fall through?

PHILIP: Er – yes.

MILLER: Well, I'm sorry about that but, quite honestly, I don't think you'll be disappointed in the long run.

PHILIP: No, I don't think I will, Maurice.

MILLER: You write a good book. We'll sell it all right.

PHILIP: (*His thoughts elsewhere*) I'm sure you will.

MILLER: I don't want to be too optimistic, of course, but – I wouldn't be surprised if we don't hit the jackpot with this idea.

PHILIP: I hope you're right.

MILLER: People are still madly interested in Teckman; you'd be surprised. Did you see that article in "The Times" yesterday?

PHILIP: No.

MILLER: It was all about Teckman, the B.109, the Garvin murder, and one of the other papers carried a most fantastic story.

PHILIP: (*Interested*) What was that?

88

MILLER: They inferred that the B.109 didn't crash, that it was stolen, in fact.

PHILIP: By Teckman?

MILLER: Well – yes.

PHILIP: In which case, Teckman is still alive?

MILLER: Yes, I suppose so. I never thought of that. (*Almost amused*) By George, if it turned out that Teckman was alive, that really would turn the book into a best-seller.

PHILIP: (*Watching MILLER*) It could indeed, Maurice. (*Suddenly*) Oh, I'm sorry – would you like a drink?

MILLER: (*Taking an envelope from his inside pocket*) I won't, if you don't mind, old boy. I'm supposed to be on my way to a cocktail party.

PHILIP: Is that the contract?

MILLER: Yes, it's only a draft; if there's anything you don't like, we can change it.

PHILIP: (*Taking the envelope from MILLER*) Fine! (*He puts the envelope in his pocket*) Maurice, you knew Teckman, didn't you?

MILLER: Only slightly.

PHILIP: Was he interested in politics?

MILLER: Politics?

PHILIP: Yes.

MILLER: Haven't the slightest idea. Look, Philip, Barbara Jefferies has got quite a lot of dope on Teckman. I'll get her to pass it over to you.

PHILIP: I'd be grateful if you would. How is she, by the way?

MILLER: Well, the last I heard she was much better.

PHILIP: Jefferies came to see me this morning …

MILLER: Oh, did he?

PHILIP: Unfortunately, I was out.

MILLER:	(*Looking at his watch*) Well, if you'll excuse me, I'll be making a move, Philip.
PHILIP:	Of course.
MILLER:	Oh, by the way, do you know a man called Harris?
PHILIP:	(*Surprised*) Why, yes.
MILLER:	What do you know about him?
PHILIP:	He's investigating the Garvin murder.
MILLER:	Is he M.I.5?
PHILIP:	Oh, I wouldn't know about that, Maurice. But why are you interested in Major Harris?
MILLER:	For a very good reason – he's interested in me.
PHILIP:	Really?
MILLER:	Well, he put me through a minor third degree, if that's anything to go by.
PHILIP:	But why should he do that? He surely doesn't think that you had anything to do with the murder?
MILLER:	(*A shrug*) I knew Teckman, I'd met Garvin, and I'm a friend of yours. I suppose that makes me some sort of suspect.
PHILIP:	(*Puzzled*) I suppose it does.

The telephone starts to ring.

MILLER:	Well, I must be toddling! I'll give you a ring tomorrow, Philip – after you've read the contract.
PHILIP:	Yes, all right. Can you let yourself out?
MILLER:	Yes, of course.

MILLER goes. PHILIP picks up the telephone.

PHILIP:	(*On phone*) Hello?
RUTH's VOICE:	(*On the other end*) Hello? Is that Mr Philip Chance?
PHILIP:	Yes, speaking …

RUTH's VOICE: Oh, good evening. My name is Ruth Wade. I telephoned you last night Mr Chance but …

PHILIP: Oh, yes, of course! I'm sorry Miss Wade, but unfortunately, I wasn't feeling very well last night …

RUTH's VOICE: Oh, that's all right …

PHILIP: What can I do for you?

CUT TO: RUTH on the telephone.

RUTH: I understand you're going to write a book about Martin Teckman?

PHILIP's VOICE: (*Surprised*) Who told you that?

RUTH: Is it true?

PHILIP's VOICE: Yes, it is, but –

RUTH: Well, if it's true, Mr Chance, I think we ought to meet. (*A note of tenseness*) There's quite a lot I can tell you about Teckman.

CUT back to PHILIP.

PHILIP: Was he a friend of yours?

RUTH's VOICE: Yes, a – very close friend.

PHILIP: All right, Miss Wade – when would you suggest?

RUTH's VOICE: Sometime this evening?

PHILIP: Well – where are you?

RUTH's VOICE: I'm in Harrison Court. It's just off Marylebone High Street. Number 47.

PHILIP: (*A momentary hesitation*) All right. I'll be there about half past nine.

RUTH's VOICE: Thank you. Goodbye.

PHILIP: (*Thoughtfully*) Goodbye.

PHILIP replaces the receiver.

CUT TO: The Front Door of No 47, Harrison Court.

PHILIP arrives, wearing a homburg hat and carrying a walking stick. A radio is playing inside the flat. PHILIP pushes the doorbell. There is no reply. After a pause he presses the bell again. He looks round the corridor then notices that the door is slightly ajar. He pushes the door with his stick; it slowly opens. PHILIP hesitates, then enters the flat.

CUT TO: The interior of the flat.

It is a modern flat; conventionally furnished. Long, full length curtains cover the windows.

PHILIP enters the lounge. He looks round and notices a half-smoked cigarette in the ashtray. The radio is playing. He moves round the room, slowly taking stock of his surroundings. He turns, glances across at the curtains: they have moved slightly, and he has noticed the movement. He walks away from the window carefully keeping his eye on the curtains. He turns and walks slowly back towards the window. He glances down and notices the toe of a girl's shoe protruding underneath the curtain. He hesitates, then tiptoes to the window; suddenly he grips the curtain and pulls it back. HELEN is standing behind the curtain holding a revolver. It is pointing at PHILIP.

END OF EPISODE THREE

EPISODE FOUR

A CABLE FROM KESNER

OPEN TO: The Interior of 47 Harrison Court.

PHILIP has just pulled back the curtain to reveal HELEN TECKMAN standing there holding a revolver. It is pointing at PHILIP.

PHILIP: Helen!

HELEN: (*Lowering the revolver*) Philip! What are you doing here?

During the following scene HELEN and PHILIP speak softly, tensely, not wishing to be overheard.

PHILIP: (*Puzzled*) I received a phone call from a girl called Ruth Wade. She said she wanted to see me, and she gave me this address.

HELEN: Did she say what she wanted to see you about?

PHILIP: Yes, of course.

HELEN: Was it about – my brother?

PHILIP: (*Nodding*) Yes. She said she knew I was writing a biography of Martin Teckman and since she was a friend of his there was quite a lot she could tell me about him.

HELEN: (*Puzzled*) This is extraordinary! I just don't understand it …

PHILIP: Why? What is it, Helen?

HELEN: Well, about half an hour after you left me, I received a telephone call from Miss Wade. She told me that she was the secretary of Sir Charles Shaughnessy and that …

PHILIP: (*Surprised*) What!

HELEN: Didn't you know that?

PHILIP: No, I hadn't the slightest idea who she was.

HELEN: I imagine it's that dark girl; the rather pretty little girl that came into the office.

PHILIP: (*Quietly*) Go on, Helen …

HELEN: Well, she said that if I came here this evening, I'd meet a very dear friend of mine. I asked her

95

	who the friend was, but she couldn't tell me over the telephone; then she gave me this address and told me not to say anything to anyone.
PHILIP:	You thought it was your brother?

HELEN nods.

PHILIP:	Well – why this? (*He points to the revolver*)
HELEN:	Just as I left the flat, I remembered that I had an old revolver of Martin's and I thought I'd bring it along just – well, just in case. When I got here, a few moments ago, the door was open and since I couldn't get any reply …
PHILIP:	(*Smiling*) You decided to investigate?
HELEN:	Yes. I got scared when I heard someone coming and hid behind the curtain.
PHILIP:	Yes – well, where is Miss Wade?
HELEN:	I – I don't know.
PHILIP:	(*Touching her arm*) Helen, you're shaking.
HELEN:	Yes, I know. (*Holding out the revolver*) Do – do you think you could take care of this?
PHILIP:	(*Faintly amused*) Yes, of course. (*Takes the revolver*) Look, this may have nothing whatever to do with your brother. The girl probably overheard our conversation with Sir Charles, and she's got some high-falutin …
HELEN:	Then why should she telephone me? And who's this 'dear friend' of mine?
PHILIP:	I don't know. (*Suddenly*) Unless of course it's me!
HELEN:	Oh, surely not!
PHILIP:	Well, I'm here! And there's no one else!
HELEN:	But I've only known you a few days, you're not exactly a very dear friend.
PHILIP:	Thank you, Miss Teckman!

HELEN:	Oh, I didn't mean that! I meant …
PHILIP:	(*Smiling*) I know what you meant. (*Takes HELEN by the arm*) Look, Helen, I'll tell you what I want you to do. I want you to go back to my flat and wait for me.
HELEN:	But what about Miss Wade?
PHILIP:	I'll deal with Miss Wade – always providing she turns up, of course.
HELEN:	Oh, but I couldn't do that – I should …
PHILIP:	You could and you're going to! (*He takes a key from his pocket*) Now take this key – please, Helen.

HELEN hesitates then takes the key.

PHILIP:	I'll come straight back to the flat as soon as I've seen Miss Wade. If she doesn't turn up in half an hour, I'll come anyway.

HELEN nods; she is obviously under a definite strain: almost shaking with nervousness.

PHILIP:	(*Watching HELEN*) Are you going to be all right?
HELEN:	Yes, I – think so.
PHILIP:	You'll find some brandy in the flat; there's a decanter on the small table. Help yourself.
HELEN:	Do you think this is a good idea, my going like this?
PHILIP:	Yes, I do.
HELEN:	(*Nodding*) All right, Philip.
PHILIP:	I shan't be long.

HELEN goes. PHILIP looks round the flat; suddenly he realises that he is holding the revolver – hesitates, then decides to put it in his pocket. He crosses to the radio and after a moment's hesitation switches it off. He returns, takes out his cigarette case: suddenly he hears someone coming and

replaces the case in his pocket. RUTH WADE enters. She is
carrying a small bottle of milk.

RUTH: (*Pleasantly surprised*) Why, hello, Mr Chance!

PHILIP: Miss Wade?

RUTH: Yes.

PHILIP: I hope you'll excuse my walking in like this. I
          couldn't make anyone hear. The door was open so
          …

RUTH: Yes, I've just been upstairs to borrow a bottle of
          milk from a neighbour of mine. (*Smiling*) I'm glad
          you made yourself at home. (*Crossing the room*)
          Will you excuse me while I pop this in the fridge?

PHILIP: (*Puzzled*) Yes, of course.

RUTH: I don't know why it is, I never seem to have
          enough milk.

RUTH goes into the kitchen. PHILIP stands looking at the
kitchen door; obviously puzzled. After a moment RUTH returns.

RUTH: It was awfully nice of you to come, Mr Chance. I
          do appreciate it.

PHILIP: We met this afternoon, didn't we?

RUTH: That's right. I'm Sir Charles Shaughnessy's
          secretary …

PHILIP: (*Bluntly; a shade unfriendly*) What is it you want to
          see me about?

RUTH: (*Faintly surprised by PHILIP's tone*) I told you
          over the telephone; about Martin Teckman.

PHILIP: I gather he was a friend of yours?

RUTH: Yes, he was.

PHILIP: (*Significantly*) A very dear friend?

RUTH: (*Quite simply; facing him*) Yes, a very dear friend,
          Mr Chance. (*Still friendly*) Can I offer you a drink?

PHILIP: No, thank you.

RUTH: (*Crossing to the table*) Well – a cigarette?

PHILIP: No, thank you.

RUTH takes a cigarette from the box; picks up a lighter; looks at PHILIP as she lights her cigarette.

RUTH: Why are you writing a book about Martin Teckman?

PHILIP: My publisher suggested it and it seemed to me a very good idea.

RUTH: Did you ever meet him?

PHILIP: No; but his sister is a friend of mine.

RUTH: (*Quietly*) So I gather. (*A moment*) Mr Chance, did you believe that story of Sir Charles?

PHILIP: I believe that he very nearly knocked a man down with his car and he thought the man was Martin Teckman.

RUTH: But you don't think it was?

PHILIP: Surely Teckman's dead: he was killed when the B.109 crashed.

RUTH: Is that what Miss Teckman thinks?

PHILIP: Obviously; it's what everyone thinks.

RUTH: (*Shaking her head*) Not everyone. (*Tensely; facing PHILIP*) I don't think Teckman is dead, in fact I'm sure he isn't.

PHILIP: What makes you so sure?

RUTH: (*A moment; curious*) Mr Chance, you don't like me, do you?

PHILIP: I don't know whether I like you or not. We hardly know each other.

RUTH: Yet, despite the fact that we hardly know each other, I sense a certain antagonism. Why?

PHILIP: (*Ignoring her question*) Did Sir Charles tell you about the car incident?

RUTH: No.

PHILIP: You overheard our conversation?

RUTH: Yes.

PHILIP: Do you make a point of listening to other people's conversations?

RUTH: Only when they concern my husband.

PHILIP: (*Astonished*) Your husband?

RUTH: Yes, my husband, Mr Chance. Martin Teckman and I were married on June 3rd, 1952. Three weeks before he tested the B.109.

PHILIP: But why doesn't Helen know about this, surely …

RUTH: We didn't want Helen to know, we didn't want anyone to know about it. I'm only telling you now because …

PHILIP: Because what, Miss Wade?

RUTH: Because if I don't take you completely into my confidence I can hardly expect you to do the same.

PHILIP: (*Quietly*) What is it you want to know?

RUTH: Apart from the story that Sir Charles told you, have you any reason to believe that my husband isn't dead?

A moment.

PHILIP: Yes. Helen received a mysterious telephone call; she seemed to think it was from Martin.

RUTH: (*Quickly; tensely*) When was this?

PHILIP: Last night.

RUTH: (*Quickly*) Did she tell you about the call?

PHILIP: I happened to be with her at the time.

RUTH: Was she convinced that it was Martin?

PHILIP: (*Puzzled by RUTH's sincerity*) Yes.

RUTH: (*Tensely*) I knew it! I knew Martin was alive! I told Helen that …

PHILIP: (*Interrupting her*) Miss Wade, if you're telling me the truth, then why hasn't Martin telephoned you – after all, you're his wife.

RUTH: Because he doesn't want me to know that he's alive.

100

PHILIP: Why not?

RUTH: (*Shaking her head*) I'm sorry, I can't answer that question.

PHILIP: You mean you won't answer it.

RUTH: I'm sorry.

PHILIP: You said just now that Helen didn't know anything about your relationship with her brother.

RUTH: Yes.

PHILIP: Why is that?

RUTH: Martin particularly didn't want his sister to know that we were married.

PHILIP: Didn't your husband get on very well with his sister?

RUTH: I don't know. I never asked him.

PHILIP: (*Quietly*) I see. Have you ever met Miss Teckman?

RUTH: No, and I've no desire to.

PHILIP: Then why did you invite her here?

RUTH: (*A puzzled frown*) Who?

PHILIP: Helen Teckman.

RUTH: I'm sorry, I don't understand.

PHILIP: It's quite a simple question, Miss Wade. You say you didn't want to talk to Helen Teckman; you didn't want her to know that you were married to her brother – in short, you didn't want to have anything to do with her.

RUTH: Yes.

PHILIP: Then why did you invite her here?

RUTH: But I didn't! Whatever gave you that idea?

PHILIP: You didn't phone Miss Teckman and ask her to come round and see you, here, tonight?

RUTH: No, of course I didn't! Did she tell you that I did?

PHILIP: Yes …

RUTH: It's quite untrue.

PHILIP: (*Slowly; watching RUTH*) She was here when I arrived.

RUTH: Then where is she now?

PHILIP: I told her to go back to my flat and wait for me.

RUTH: While you dealt with Miss Wade?

PHILIP: Yes.

RUTH: I see. (*She looks at PHILIP; obviously tense*) Well, it's perfectly simple, isn't it, Mr Chance? Obviously, one of us is lying. (*Stubbing out her cigarette in an ashtray*) It's up to you to decide which.

CUT TO: The Drawing Room of PHILIP's flat.

HELEN TECKMAN is stubbing out a cigarette in an ashtray. She is wearing a lucky charm bracelet. She is obviously a little worried: faintly on edge. She has a small glass of brandy in her hand. The doorbell rings and HELEN puts down the glass and crosses to the door to admit PHILIP.

CUT TO: *Helen opening the front door: she is surprised to find herself facing MAJOR HARRIS.*

HARRIS: (*Unperturbed*) Good evening, Miss Teckman!

HELEN: Oh, hello, Major! I – I was expecting Mr Chance.

HARRIS: Isn't he in?

HELEN: No, I'm afraid not.

HARRIS: May I wait?

HELEN: Er – yes, of course.

HARRIS: Thank you.

HARRIS enters.

CUT TO: *HARRIS entering the drawing room, followed by HELEN.*

HELEN: I don't think Mr Chance will be very long.

HARRIS: I'm in no hurry.

102

HELEN: (*Rather ill at ease*) I saw him earlier this evening and he asked me to come here and wait for him.

HARRIS: Indeed.

HELEN: He gave me the key, that's how I managed to get in …

HARRIS: I didn't think you'd climbed through the window.

HELEN: (*An uneasy little laugh*) No … Er – can I get you a drink?

HARRIS: No, thank you.

HELEN: I – I was just having a sip of brandy. I haven't been feeling very well. (*She picks up her glass*)

HARRIS: Oh, I'm sorry.

HELEN: It's nothing, I just … felt faint, that's all. (*She drinks*)

HARRIS: I understand you saw Sir Charles Shaughnessy this morning?

HELEN: Yes, he asked me to go and see him.

HARRIS: Why?

HELEN: He wanted to have a talk with me.

HARRIS: About your brother?

HELEN: Yes.

HARRIS: It's surprising the number of people who seem to be interested in your brother, Miss Teckman. Did he arouse as much interest when he was alive?

HELEN: Don't you know? You seem to be one of the people who are interested in him.

HARRIS: Yes, but mine is a curious profession. I only get interested in people when they're dead – or disappear.

HELEN stretches out her hand to put her glass down on the table. The clasp on her bracelet is loose and the bracelet falls from her wrist. HARRIS stoops and picks it up.

HELEN: Oh, dear, that's always happening. I shall have to get it seen to.

HARRIS: (*Looking at the bracelet*) It's a most unusual bracelet.

HELEN: Yes.

HARRIS: I don't usually like these lucky charm bracelets, but this is most attractive. (*He hands it back to HELEN*)

HELEN: (*Trying to fasten the bracelet on her wrist*) My brother gave it to me. He bought it in Madrid, just before the War.

HARRIS: (*Watching HELEN*) Allow me …

HARRIS takes the bracelet from HELEN and slowly puts it round her wrist and fastens it. HELEN is just a shade embarrassed.

HELEN: Thank you.

(*The front doorbell rings*)

HARRIS: That sounds like Mr Chance.

HELEN: Yes.

HELEN goes out.

CUT TO: *HELEN opening the front door. PHILIP enters.*

PHILIP: I'm sorry I've been so long, but …

HELEN: (*Quietly*) Major Harris is here.

PHILIP: (*Surprised*) Major Harris?

HELEN: Yes.

PHILIP: How long has he been here?

HELEN: About two or three minutes. I think he wants to talk to you privately; I'll phone you later, Philip.

PHILIP: No, wait, Helen! I saw Miss Wade …

HELEN: (*Quickly*) What did she say?

PHILIP: Apparently, she was – a very close friend of your brother's. She heard what Sir Charles said this morning and she wanted to know if …

HELEN: Yes?

PHILIP:	Well, if you had any reason to believe that your brother was still alive.
HELEN:	What did you say?
PHILIP:	I told her about the telephone call.
HELEN:	But do you think she was telling the truth? I don't ever remember Martin mentioning anyone called Ruth.
PHILIP:	I don't know whether she was telling the truth or not. I can't make up my mind.
HELEN:	Philip, what is it? Is something worrying you?
PHILIP:	Yes. (*A moment*) She did telephone you tonight, didn't she, Helen?
HELEN:	(*Annoyed*) Why, yes, of course she did! Why do you ask?
PHILIP:	(*Softly*) She said that she didn't …
HELEN:	Why, that's a lie! What do you think I was doing at the flat if she didn't phone me? Why, I never heard of the girl until …
PHILIP:	Yes, of course.
HELEN:	(*Tensely*) Philip, you do believe me, don't you?
PHILIP:	Yes, of course I do, Helen. (*Taking hold of her arm and leading her to the door*) I'll phone you later after I've talked to Harris.
HELEN:	(*Nodding: smiling at PHILIP*) All right …
PHILIP:	Are you feeling any better?
HELEN:	Yes … (*Softly; near to PHILIP*) Phone me later … (*She goes out of the front door*)

CUT TO: The Drawing Room.

MAJOR HARRIS is examining a cigarette lighter; he puts it down on the table as PHILIP enters.

HARRIS:	Good evening.
PHILIP:	I'm sorry to have kept you waiting.

HARRIS: That's quite all right. Miss Teckman's been entertaining me.

A pause.

PHILIP: (*Not too friendly*) Well?

HARRIS: (*Smiling*) Well, Mr Chance?

PHILIP: What can I do for you?

HARRIS: Ah, yes … Well, you can start by finding me this elusive friend of yours – Mr John Rice.

PHILIP: Haven't you found him yet?

HARRIS: No, we haven't. It's odd, isn't it? We haven't even got proof of his existence.

PHILIP: But you know perfectly well that Rice exists! He gave me the cheque; he gave me a letter of introduction – he also gave me an extremely unpleasant bump on the back of the head.

HARRIS: So you say.

PHILIP: Don't you believe me?

HARRIS: I should feel happier if you could produce Mr Rice.

PHILIP: (*Angry*) Well, I can't produce him. What do you expect me to do – rub the magic lamp?

HARRIS: (*Unperturbed*) If you have a magic lamp it might be a very good idea.

PHILIP: Now look here, Harris, or whatever your name is …

HARRIS: (*Quite pleasantly*) The name is Harris.

PHILIP: Well, look here, Major Harris, I'm just a little tired of this continual cross-examination. I told you the truth about Rice – the whole truth – there's nothing else I can tell you.

HARRIS: That's unfortunate, Mr Chance.

PHILIP: Unfortunate?

HARRIS: Unless we find Rice we shall be forced to the unpleasant conclusion that he doesn't exist; in

106

which case we shall want to know who gave you that letter and why you were taking it to Berlin.

PHILIP: But I've told you why I was taking it to Berlin! Rice told me that it was a letter of introduction to a man called Rudolph Kesner. I never for one moment imagined that ... (*He stops; a sudden thought*) Just a minute! Have you tried to contact Kesner?

HARRIS: No ...

PHILIP: But surely that's the obvious thing to do!

HARRIS: (*Nodding*) Which is why we haven't done it. (*Sitting on the arm of one of the armchairs*) Mr Chance, I came here tonight because I have a suggestion to make to you.

PHILIP: Well?

HARRIS: If you're telling us the truth then obviously Rice would like to get that letter back; that's why he was here when you returned from the Airport.

PHILIP: Yes.

HARRIS: Now I understand from the Inspector that you left him with some doubt as to whether you had the letter or not.

PHILIP: Yes, I did. (*Suddenly*) Look here, how important was that letter?

HARRIS: (*Slowly*) It is a drawing of the B.109.

PHILIP: Yes, I know that. I saw it. But there's nothing secret about that; there's been drawings and photographs of the B.109 in every newspaper.

HARRIS: There has indeed. (*Almost a change in attitude*) Mr Chance, I'll tell you what I want you to do.

PHILIP: Yes.

HARRIS: I want you to send a cable to Berlin.

PHILIP: (*Surprised*) To Berlin?

HARRIS: (*Nodding*) Yes.

107

PHILIP: But why to Berlin?

HARRIS: I want you to cable Rudolph Kesner. Tell him you
            wish to contact Rice immediately and you haven't
            got his address.

HARRIS turns towards the telephone and picks up the receiver.

PHILIP: But – but do you think he'll fall for that?

*HARRIS is dialling; he listens to the ringing-out tone on the
telephone.*

HARRIS: (*Looking up*) What did you say?

PHILIP: I said, do you think he'll fall for it?

HARRIS: I hope so, Mr Chance. (*He holds the telephone
            receiver out towards PHILIP. Smiles*) For your
            sake …

CUT TO: *A young man (A G.P.O. Messenger) on a G.P.O.
motorcycle is riding down a country lane by the side of the
river. There are several river craft in the background. He gets
off his cycle near a large Houseboat and crosses to it. He leans
over the side and shouts*:

MESSENGER: Mr Rigby! Mr Rigby!

*After a moment RICE appears from below decks: he is wearing
old grey bags and a polo neck sweater. The MESSENGER
hands RICE a telegram: RICE opens it and reads the message.
We see what the telegram says: "Have Received Cable From
Philip Chance Stop He wishes to contact you Stop Kesner".
RICE looks up from the telegram and nods to the
MESSENGER.*

CUT TO: *PHILIP CHANCE is in his flat working on a
manuscript; reading, making notes: he sits at his desk; cup of
coffee on desk. He wears a dressing gown. The telephone rings.
He picks up the phone.*

PHILIP: Hello?

RICE: (*On the other end*) Hello – is that Philip Chance?

PHILIP: (*Tensely; recognising the voice*) Speaking …

RICE: Good morning, Mr Chance. I understand you've been trying to get in touch with me.

PHILIP: Who is that?

CUT TO: *RICE in a telephone box in a country lane.*

RICE: You know who it is. It's Rice.

For the rest of this conversation we cut back and forth between PHILIP and RICE.

PHILIP: Oh, hello, Rice! Yes, I wanted to see you. I cabled Kesner because I hadn't got your address.

RICE: What is it you want?

PHILIP: I was wondering if you were still interested in the letter?

RICE: (*Cautiously*) What letter?

PHILIP: The one you asked me to deliver to Mr Kesner.

RICE: Sure, I'm interested in it; but I was under the impression that you'd handed it over to the police.

PHILIP: Why should you think that?

RICE: Didn't they stop you at the Airport?

PHILIP: Yes, but I didn't give them the letter. I've still got it.

RICE: (*Hesitating; then*) Okay, you can post it to me. I'll give you the address.

PHILIP: Oh, no, Mr Rice. If you want the letter you pay for it – in cash.

RICE: How much?

PHILIP: We'll discuss that when we meet.

RICE: We don't meet!

PHILIP: All right – we don't meet, then you don't get the letter.

RICE: (*Quickly*) No, wait a minute! I'll tell you what I'll do …

PHILIP: No, Rice, I'll tell you what I'll do. I'll meet you at my Club at four o'clock this afternoon. And I suggest that …

RICE: That's impossible, I can't get up to Town.

PHILIP: Well – what do you suggest?

RICE: You'll have to come down here?

PHILIP: All right, give me the address.

A moment.

RICE: I've got a houseboat at a place called Datchet, it's near Windsor. If you ask at the local post office, they'll tell you where I am. The name, by the way, is Rigby.

PHILIP: Four o'clock this afternoon.

RICE: Okay.

RICE replaces the receiver.

CUT TO: *PHILIP also replaces his receiver. He looks thoughtful; after a moment he dials a number.*

CUT TO: *RICE comes out of the telephone box in the country lane.*

CUT TO: *RICE climbs aboard his houseboat. He goes down below to the cabin.*

CUT TO: The interior of the cabin of the houseboat. There is a table in the centre with various objects strewn about the cabin.

RICE enters and suddenly stops dead. He is obviously surprised to find someone else in the cabin, waiting for him. The visitor is out of shot and remains so.

RICE: (*Tensely*) What do you want, why have you come here? Now listen, I can explain exactly what happened when …

RICE lowers his eyes; obviously looking at a revolver in his visitor's hand.

RICE: (*Suddenly; frightened*) Don't be a fool, put that down. If you don't put it down, I'll …

RICE suddenly springs forward and there is an immediate shot. RICE staggers back; obviously hit; then he falls forward across the table.

CUT TO: *A police car in a country lane. The houseboat and river can be seen in the distance. MAJOR HARRIS, DETECTIVE-INSPECTOR HILTON, a uniform Police Driver, and a Plain Clothes Sergeant are in the car. PHILIP drives past in his car and stops a few yards away from the houseboat. He gets out of his car and climbs aboard the houseboat. He looks round; notices the hatch and the entrance to the cabin. He peers down the hatchway.*

PHILIP: (*Calling down*) … Rice! Hello, there! Rice!

CUT TO: The interior of the cabin.

The dead body of RICE is sprawled across the table: he is now holding a revolver in his right hand. The picture is one of suicide. PHILIP enters and immediately dashes to RICE and examines him; he realises that he is dead. He looks round the cabin and decides to fetch the police immediately. He crosses the cabin and then suddenly notices something on the floor. He stoops down and picks up the object. It is a lucky charm from a lucky charm bracelet. PHILIP looks puzzled; worried. He suddenly takes his handkerchief out of his breast pocket and puts the charm in it. He replaces the handkerchief in his breast pocket.

CUT TO: *The occupants of the police car are watching the houseboat. The shot is taken through the windscreen of the car. PHILIP can be seen emerging from the cabin of the houseboat.*

111

He arrives on the deck and waves excitedly to the occupants of the car.

HILTON: (*In the car*) There's something wrong! He wants us!

CUT TO: *INSPECTOR HILTON together with MAJOR HARRIS and the PLAIN-CLOTHES SERGEANT climb onto the houseboat.*

CUT TO: The interior of the cabin.

INSPECTOR HILTON enters followed by MAJOR HARRIS and PHILIP. HILTON quickly examines the body; HARRIS looks round the cabin. PHILIP stands watching the INSPECTOR.

HILTON: He's dead all right. (*To PHILIP*) Was he like this when you found him?

PHILIP: Yes.

HARRIS is looking round the cabin; not touching anything.

HARRIS: (*To HILTON*) How long do you think he's been dead?

HILTON: It's difficult to say. An hour at least. (*To PHILIP*) Did you touch anything?

PHILIP: Yes, I'm afraid I did. I wasn't sure whether he was dead.

HARRIS: You recognise him?

PHILIP: Yes. It's Rice.

HILTON: You're sure?

PHILIP: I'm absolutely sure.

HARRIS looks at HILTON.

HILTON: (*Nodding*) I'll check with the local people.

HILTON goes out. There is a pause.

PHILIP: (*Faintly nervous*) If he's been dead an hour, I suppose they've had time to get back to Town.

HARRIS: Who?

PHILIP: Why – the person who did it.

HARRIS: You don't think it was suicide?

PHILIP: No, I – don't. Do you?

HARRIS: (*Watching PHILIP*) Well, it looks like suicide, doesn't it, Mr Chance?

PHILIP: Yes, I know, but – why should Rice commit suicide? He sounded all right on the phone; besides he was expecting me with the letter.

HARRIS: Perhaps he didn't trust you.

PHILIP: Well, even so, he surely wouldn't commit suicide.

HARRIS: You wouldn't think so. You haven't any other reason for thinking it wasn't suicide, have you, Mr Chance?

PHILIP: Why, no, of course not. Why do you ask?

HARRIS: I wondered that's all.

Nervously, and without thinking, PHILIP puts his hand on his breast pocket.

CUT TO: *PHILIP's car drives up to a telephone box in a country lane. PHILIP gets out of the car and goes into the box. He dials for the operator.*

CUT TO: *The telephone on the table in HELEN's flat is ringing. HELEN picks it up: she is wearing her lucky charm bracelet. For the duration of this conversation, we cut back and forth between HELEN and PHILIP.*

HELEN: (*On phone*) Hello?

PHILIP: (*On the other end*) Hello – is that you, Helen?

HELEN: Yes …

PHILIP: This is Philip …

HELEN: Oh, hello, Philip!

PHILIP: (*Nervously*) Helen, I've been trying to get you; I phoned you an hour ago but there was no reply.

HELEN: Really? That's extraordinary! I've been in the whole afternoon.

PHILIP: Are you sure?

HELEN: Yes, of course I'm sure.

PHILIP: Oh – perhaps I got the wrong number.

HELEN: Philip, what is it?

PHILIP: Something's happened – something very important – I've got to see you.

HELEN: (*Puzzled*) Yes, all right. Would you like to have dinner with me tonight, here, at the flat?

PHILIP: No, I'm sorry, I can't – not tonight. I'm supposed to be dining with Miller. Can you come round to my place?

HELEN: Yes, of course. Straight away?

PHILIP: No, in about an hour's time.

HELEN: Yes, all right, Philip.

PHILIP: Goodbye.

HELEN: Goodbye!

HELEN slowly replaces the receiver; she looks very puzzled.

CUT TO: The Drawing Room of PHILIP's flat.

MRS LACEY enters from the kitchen with several pieces of silver which she has been cleaning. She is arranging it as PHILIP enters, he wears an overcoat and carries his hat. His manner is tense, on edge.

MRS LACEY: Oh, good afternoon, sir.

PHILIP: Hello, Mrs Lacey. Any messages?

MRS LACEY: Yes. Mr Miller telephoned, sir. He wants you to meet him at the (*Puzzled*) something mayonnaise.

PHILIP: The what?

MRS LACEY: The something mayonnaise.

PHILIP: Well, what's that?

MRS LACEY: I don't know, sir. It sounded very French, sir.

PHILIP: Oh! The Auberge D'Armaille!

MRS LACEY: That's it! I couldn't quite catch it!

114

PHILIP: It's a restaurant, Mrs Lacey. Did Mr Miller say what time?

MRS LACEY: Yes – half-past seven, sir.

PHILIP: Thank you. Nothing else?

MRS LACEY: No, sir.

MRS LACEY goes into the kitchen. PHILIP takes out the handkerchief and produces the lucky charm. He crosses to the table lamp; switches it on and examines the lucky charm under the light. The doorbell rings. PHILIP looks up. MRS LACEY enters and crosses to the front door. PHILIP puts the lucky charm in his pocket. MRS LACEY returns with HELEN.

MRS LACEY: Miss Teckman, sir.

PHILIP: Come in, Helen!

MRS LACEY goes into the kitchen.

HELEN: Have you just got in?

PHILIP: Yes. Let me take your things.

HELEN: No, it's all right. Philip, what's happened? You sounded terribly worried over the phone.

PHILIP: Helen, listen – you told me that you'd been in your flat the whole afternoon. Is that true?

HELEN: Yes, of course it is.

PHILIP: And this morning?

HELEN: I went out for about an hour, that's all. (*Anxiously*) Philip, what is it?

PHILIP: (*A moment*) They've found Rice.

HELEN: When?

PHILIP: This afternoon.

HELEN: Where?

PHILIP: He's been living on a houseboat near Windsor. He called himself Rigby.

HELEN: But this is good news, isn't it? Now the police are bound to believe that …

PHILIP: Rice is dead! He was murdered.

HELEN: (*Softly*) Oh, Philip! What – what happened?

115

PHILIP:	He was shot. I found the body in the cabin. It looked like suicide but …
HELEN:	(*Alarmed*) You found the body!
PHILIP:	Yes …
HELEN:	Philip! They don't think that you murdered him?
PHILIP:	No! No, of course not.
HELEN:	(*Bewildered*) Well, what is it? What's the matter?
PHILIP:	(*Taking the lucky charm out of his pocket*) I found this on the floor, near the body. It's off your bracelet …
HELEN:	(*Stunned*) What!
PHILIP:	(*Quietly; watching her*) It's a lucky charm, Helen. It's off your bracelet.

HELEN looks quickly at her bracelet then looks up to PHILIP.

HELEN:	(*A shade annoyed*) What on earth do you mean?
PHILIP:	(*Suddenly; puzzled*) Well – isn't it?
HELEN:	No, of course it isn't!

HELEN holds out her hand towards PHILIP.

| HELEN: | You can see for yourself – there's nothing missing. |

PHILIP looks down at the bracelet; puzzled.

| HELEN: | (*Staring at PHILIP; surprised and rather annoyed*) Whatever made you think it was off my bracelet? |

CUT TO: A corner table in a small restaurant in Greek Street. The table is situated almost in the apex of a triangle: a large window on one side of the table and a wall on the other.

The MAN we have seen in Episode One and at the end of Episode Two is sitting at the table. There is a glass of sherry in front of him. He is alone, but it is a table for two. The MAN

116

suddenly notices the person he is waiting for and calls across the room.

MAN: Mr Chance!

PHILIP is standing inside the curtained alcove entrance into the restaurant. He is puzzled by the fact that the stranger is smiling at him and beckoning him. He moves towards the table.

PHILIP: Did you call me?

MAN: Yes, I did. (*Smiling*) It is Philip Chance, isn't it?

PHILIP: (*Puzzled*) Yes.

MAN: Mr Miller asked me to tell you that he's unavoidably delayed.

PHILIP: (*Faintly annoyed*) Oh …

MAN: (*Smiling*) He asked me to entertain you for a quarter of an hour or so.

PHILIP: Oh, I see.

MAN: Won't you sit down?

PHILIP: (*After a momentary hesitation*) Thank you.

MAN: Can I offer you a drink?

PHILIP: Mr – may I have a sherry?

MAN: Yes, of course.

The MAN beckons to a WAITER who is out of the picture.

PHILIP: (*Taking stock of his companion*) I don't think we've met before, have we, Mr –?

MAN: No, we haven't.

PHILIP: Are you a friend of Maurice's?

MAN: No. (*After a tiny pause; quietly*) But I'm a friend of yours, Mr Chance.

PHILIP: What do you mean? (*Suddenly; suspicious*) Who are you?

MAN: I'm Martin Teckman.

END OF EPISODE FOUR

EPISODE FIVE

MARTIN TECKMAN

OPEN TO: *PHILIP CHANCE and MARTIN TECKMAN (THE MAN) are sitting at the table in the Greek Street Restaurant.*

MAN: Can I offer you a drink?

PHILIP: Mr – may I have a sherry?

MAN: Yes, of course.

The MAN beckons to a WAITER who is out of the picture.

PHILIP: (*Taking stock of his companion*) I don't think we've met before, have we, Mr –?

MAN: No, we haven't.

PHILIP: Are you a friend of Maurice's?

MAN: No. (*After a tiny pause; quietly*) But I'm a friend of yours, Mr Chance.

PHILIP: What do you mean? (*Suddenly; suspicious*) Who are you?

MAN: I'm Martin Teckman.

PHILIP: (*Astonished*) Martin Teckman!

MAN: Yes … Don't you believe me?

PHILIP stares at TECKMAN, then suddenly rises.

MAN: (*Quickly*) Where are you going?

PHILIP: I'm going for the police!

MAN: Sit down!

PHILIP hesitates.

MAN: Sit down, please!

PHILIP slowly sits down; still staring at the MAN. The WAITER arrives.

WAITER: (*To MAN*) Yes, sir?

MAN: A sherry for my friend.

WAITER: (*To PHILIP*) A dry sherry, sir?

PHILIP ignores the WAITER and keeps his eyes on TECKMAN. The MAN nods to the WAITER who goes.

MAN: Well, Mr Chance, you've had a good look – do you believe me?

PHILIP: (*Quietly; still watching him*) Yes, you're Martin Teckman, all right.

121

MAN: Good. That's over the first obstacle, anyway.
         (*Smiles*) I was worried about that. I thought, look
         well if I can't convince him I'm Teckman, then I'm
         really sunk.

PHILIP: What is it you want?

MAN: Well, first of all I want to ask you a few questions,
         and then I want you to do me a little favour.

PHILIP: (*A shade angry*) If there's any questions to be
         asked, I'm the person who's going to ask them!

MAN: (*Quietly*) All right. Fair enough. We'll both ask
         questions. But why the antagonism? You can
         hardly dislike me, surely – we've never met
         before!

PHILIP: It's curious you should say that; someone else said
         almost exactly the same thing to me.

MAN: Oh. Who was that?

PHILIP: Your wife.

MAN: (*After a moment; tensely*) I haven't got a wife.

PHILIP: Really? There seems to be a difference of opinion
         on that point.

MAN: I didn't ask you here to discuss my wife.

PHILIP: You didn't ask me here at all. I'm supposed to be
         dining with my publisher.

MAN: Yes, I apologise about that. I called round to see
         you just as Miller telephoned. I heard your
         housekeeper mention this restaurant so I …

PHILIP: Go on …

MAN: So I left a message at Miller's office saying you'd
         be here at eight o'clock instead of seven-thirty.

PHILIP: I see.

MAN: (*Suddenly; tense, yet friendly*) Chance, listen – I
         wouldn't have taken this risk if I hadn't have been
         desperate. I want to know what happened to
         Andrew?

122

PHILIP: (*Puzzled*) Andrew?

MAN: Andrew Garvin. He was murdered. They found him in your flat.

PHILIP: Yes.

MAN: Well – what happened? Why your flat?

PHILIP: Two interesting questions, Mr Teckman. But what about the third question – who murdered him?

MAN: (*Quietly*) I think I know who murdered him.

PHILIP: I suspected that.

MAN: (*Leaning forward*) Chance, listen. I haven't a lot of time. What was Andrew doing in your flat?

PHILIP: I don't know.

MAN: (*Suddenly, tensely, leaning forward across the table*) Are you one of them? Is that why you refuse to tell me about Andrew …

PHILIP: (*Angry; interrupting*) What are you talking about?

MAN: Andrew Garvin was a friend of mine – a very dear friend. I know why he was murdered, and I've got a pretty shrewd idea who murdered him, but I don't understand what he was doing in your flat!

PHILIP: Neither do I, Mr Teckman.

MAN: Yes, but did you know Andrew? Had you met him?

PHILIP: (*Nodding*) I'd interviewed him. My publisher asked me to write your biography and he suggested that I had a chat with Garvin. He said Garvin knew more about you than anyone else.

MAN: And it was after you interviewed Garvin that he was murdered?

PHILIP: Yes. Whether he came up to Town to see me or not, I don't know. I'd been to my club for the afternoon. When I got home – he was there.

MAN: Was he dead when you found him?

PHILIP: Yes.

MAN: You say that Maurice Miller told you to go and see Andrew?

PHILIP: He suggested it.

MAN: (*Nodding: thoughtfully*) Yes, he would. He knew I was a great friend of Andrew's. I knew Miller during the War. We were in the RAF together. I expect that was one of the reasons why he wanted to publish my biography.

PHILIP: Yes, I think it was. That and the fact that, like everyone else, he was interested in you and the B.109.

MAN: What did Andrew tell you about the B.109?

PHILIP: He had a theory, and apparently not such a stupid one after all. He didn't believe that the plane did disintegrate, he thought ... (*Hesitates*)

MAN: Well?

PHILIP: He thought it landed somewhere; he thought the wreckage has been planted.

TECKMAN looks down at the table; moves one of the knives.

PHILIP: Is that what happened?

MAN: No – fortunately.

PHILIP: Then what did happen?

MAN: (*Looking up; a suggestion of a smile*) Shall we say, I changed my mind?

PHILIP: (*Quietly; stunned*) You mean Garvin was right, that was the original plan, but –

MAN: (*Tensely*) But I changed my mind, let's leave it at that.

A moment.

PHILIP: Teckman, what did you mean just now when you said you were not a friend of Miller's – but a friend of mine?

MAN: I meant I wanted to give you a piece of advice, good advice ...

124

PHILIP: Well?

MAN: Get on a plane first thing tomorrow morning – get on it and stay on it!

PHILIP: Why should I do that?

MAN: If you don't, you'll end up like Andrew Garvin.

PHILIP: But why? Why should anyone want to murder me?

MAN: Because you're interested in Martin Teckman, that's why.

PHILIP: (*Leaning forward; almost aggressive*) Look, Teckman, I'm a novelist. Until I got mixed up in this business, I led a lazy, sophisticated, irresponsible existence and I loved every minute of it! I want to go back to that way of living as quickly as I can, but I don't intend to until I know exactly what this is all about. Now question number one! Where were you taking the B.109?

MAN: I'll give you one guess.

PHILIP: All right. Why did you change your mind?

MAN: I suddenly discovered a streak of sentimentality in my nature that I didn't know existed. I realised that I was ideologically unsound and devoted to bourgeois inefficiency. In short – I grew up.

PHILIP: (*Quietly*) What happened?

MAN: I baled out. I intended it to be not only the end of the B.109, but the end of Martin Teckman. For the first eighteen months, I got away with it, then one day – quite by accident – someone saw me. I knew then that the game was up. Twenty-four hours later a man was shot. Do you know why he was shot?

PHILIP: No.

MAN: He was wearing the wrong overcoat; they thought it was me.

125

PHILIP: Yes, but look here, Teckman, why should these people want to kill you? If you did a deal with them …

MAN: (*Interrupting*) Because I know too much. I know who they are, what they are, and how they work. (*Angry*) But what the fools don't realise is, if they'd left me alone, I'd have done nothing about it. If I'd wanted to have talked, I could have done it in the first week.

PHILIP: Why didn't you?

MAN: Sentimentality is no substitute for courage, Mr Chance.

PHILIP: Yes, well, you're going to talk now! I'm taking you straight to Inspector Hilton.

MAN: Unfortunately, it isn't quite as simple as that. (*He takes a letter from his pocket*) Chance, I want you to do me a favour … (*He holds the letter up; turns it round between his fingers*)

PHILIP: Well?

MAN: Will you please give this letter to my sister?

The WAITER arrives with the sherry.

PHILIP: Yes, of course I will, but I still insist that you …

PHILIP stops on seeing the WAITER.

WAITER: Excuse me, sir. You're wanted on the telephone.

PHILIP: (*Surprised*) I am?

WAITER: Yes, sir. (*He indicates another part of the room*) It's in the alcove, sir.

The WAITER puts the glass of sherry down on the table. PHILIP rises, looks at TECKMAN, hesitates, then moves out of the screen. As soon as PHILIP has gone, TECKMAN rises, nods to the WAITER, and gives him a pound note. He puts the letter down on the table.

MAN: Don't let him forget this.

WAITER: No, sir.

126

CUT TO: PHILIP in the telephone box.

PHILIP: (*On phone ... Impatiently*) Hello? … Hello? …
(*There is no reply from the other end*) …Hello? …
Confound it! Hello? (*He flicks the receiver*) Hello?

Suddenly it dawns on PHILIP that this is probably a ruse to get him away from the table; he quickly replaces the receiver.

CUT BACK to the table.

The MAN has gone. The WAITER is re-arranging the knives and forks. PHILIP arrives.

PHILIP: Where is he?

WAITER: I beg your pardon, sir?

PHILIP: (*Urgently; angry*) Where is he? Where's the man who was sitting at this table?

WAITER: He's just left, sir.

PHILIP rushes towards the curtained entrance into the restaurant and bumps into MAURICE MILLER who is just entering.

MILLER: Philip!

PHILIP: I'll be with you in a minute, Maurice!

MILLER: (*Grabbing PHILIP by the arm; detaining him*) Philip, what's happened? What is it?

PHILIP: (*Pulling himself free*) I'll explain later!

PHILIP dashes out. Somewhat bewildered, MILLER turns towards the WAITER.

MILLER: What on earth is going on here?

WAITER: (*A shade worried*) I don't know, sir.

MILLER: (*Puzzled*) Well, where's he gone to? Is he chasing someone?

WAITER: There was a gentleman at the table, sir. He decided to leave. I don't really know what happened, sir.

MILLER crosses to the table.

MILLER: Is this where they were sitting?

WAITER: Yes, sir.

MILLER: (*Picking up the letter*) Well, what's this?

WAITER: The first gentleman left it, sir – he said it was for your friend.

MILLER looks at the letter; after a moment he looks up.

MILLER: All right, I'll take care of it. Fetch me a gin and French.

WAITER: Yes, sir.

The WAITER goes. MILLER sits at the table and looks at the letter again. PHILIP returns through the curtained entrance. He looks agitated and slightly out of breath. He suddenly sees MILLER and crosses to the table. MILLER rises. The letter is now on the table.

MILLER: Philip, for goodness sake, what's this all about?

PHILIP: I've seen Teckman! He was here, at the table, waiting for me.

MILLER: (*Astonished*) Teckman? You don't mean …

PHILIP: (*Tensely*) Yes, Martin Teckman. Now listen, Maurice – this is what I want you to do …

MILLER: But you must be mistaken! Teckman's dead! He was killed when the …

PHILIP: Teckman's alive – very much alive!

MILLER: But I don't see how he can be!

PHILIP: Maurice, please! You've got to listen to me, this is very important! I want you to go back to my flat and phone Inspector Hilton at Scotland Yard. If he isn't there find out where you can get in touch with him. I must see Hilton tonight – it's very urgent.

MILLER: Yes, all right, Philip.

PHILIP: (*Picking up the letter*) I'm taking this round to Helen Teckman. I'll join you at the flat later.

MILLER: (*Baffled but catching some of PHILIP's excitement*) Philip, are you serious? Was it Teckman?

128

PHILIP: (*Nodding*) It was Teckman all right!

CUT TO: The Drawing Room of HELEN TECKMAN's flat.
The telephone is ringing. HELEN enters and lifts the receiver. For the duration of this conversation, we cut back and forth between HELEN in her flat and PHILIP who is in a telephone box.

HELEN: (*On phone*) Hello?
PHILIP: (*On the other end*) Hello, is that you, Helen?
HELEN: Oh, hello, Philip!
PHILIP: Oh, good, I was afraid you might be out! Are you alone?
HELEN: Yes.
PHILIP: I've got to see you. It's very urgent. I'm coming round straight away.
HELEN: What is it? What's happened?
PHILIP: I've got a letter for you – it's from your brother.
HELEN: (*Astonished*) From Martin?
PHILIP: Yes, I'm in Greek Street at the moment. I'll be with you as soon as I can pick up a cab.
HELEN: Philip, what's happened? Did you see him? Did you talk to him?
PHILIP: Yes, I'll tell you all about it when I see you.
PHILIP replaces the receiver.

CUT TO: The Drawing Room of HELEN's flat. There are drinks, cigarettes, etc on the table.
HELEN is waiting for PHILIP; she is tense, a shade overwrought, and is smoking a cigarette. She stubs out the cigarette in an ashtray. She looks at her wristlet watch. Suddenly the doorbell rings and HELEN rushes out to answer it. We hear the sound of the front door opening and closing. PHILIP comes in followed by HELEN who is obviously excited.

HELEN: Philip, what happened? Are you sure it was Martin?

PHILIP: (*Taking the letter out of his pocket*) Yes, we had a long talk; he asked me to give you this letter. (*He takes hold of HELEN's arm; faces her*) Helen, before I give it to you, there's something I've got to know.

HELEN: Well? Well – what is it?

A pause.

PHILIP: Do you know the truth about your brother? Have you known it all along?

HELEN: (*A moment: distressed*) I've had my suspicions. You asked me once whether he was mixed up in politics, but I evaded the question, do you remember? I think that's why I disliked Andrew Garvin …

PHILIP: Because he knew about Martin?

HELEN: Yes, it hurt me to think that someone even suspected him.

PHILIP: Your brother had instructions to fly the B.109 to a secret base, did you know that?

HELEN: Oh, no! No, I don't believe it!

PHILIP: It's true. Fortunately, he changed his mind.

HELEN: Did he tell you that?

PHILIP: Yes.

HELEN: (*Holding PHILIP's arm; distressed*) Oh, Philip!

PHILIP: (*Giving HELEN the letter*) He's in danger …

HELEN: (*Softly*) Yes, I know …

PHILIP: They've been searching for him for eighteen months; but he's been lucky. He can't go on like that, Helen. We've got to find him and hand him over to the police.

HELEN: Yes.

130

HELEN looks down at the letter she is holding; after a moment she tears open the envelope, then hesitates. She takes hold of PHILIP's arm in order to steady herself.

PHILIP: Are you feeling faint?

HELEN: Yes. I'll – I'll be all right in a moment.

PHILIP: Can I get you anything?

HELEN: No, no, I don't think so.

HELEN takes a folded sheet of notepaper out of the envelope.

PHILIP: I'll get you a drink!

PHILIP moves to the table and pours HELEN a small glass of brandy. He returns to HELEN.

PHILIP: Here, drink this …

HELEN: No, I'll be all right …

PHILIP: Helen, please!

HELEN takes the glass and drinks. PHILIP looks at the note she is holding.

HELEN: (*Offering PHILIP the note*) Read it to me …

PHILIP: (*Hesitating*) Are you sure it's not personal, because …?

HELEN: (*Shaking her head*) No … Read it … Please!

PHILIP looks at HELEN then slowly unfolds the note; he looks at it and after a moment he reads:

PHILIP: (*Reading*) "Dear Helen … What can I say to you? Except to ask your forgiveness? Try not to think too badly of me. I realise now of course that my wife influenced me; without her influence all this could never have happened … If only I'd taken Andrew's advice … Take care of yourself, Helen. God bless. Martin." …

HELEN: (*Taking the note from PHILIP and staring at it*) What does he mean – "His wife"? (*Looking up; astonished*) Is Martin married?

PHILIP: Yes.

HELEN: (*Softly; near to tears*) Did you know?

PHILIP: Yes. His wife told me. (*After a tiny pause*)
                 He's married to Ruth Wade.

HELEN looks puzzled and distressed.

CUT TO: The Drawing Room of PHILIP's flat.

MAURICE MILLER is glancing through the pages of a magazine, but he is obviously not interested in it. The doorbell rings and MRS LACEY comes out of the kitchen and crosses to the door. MILLER stands watching her. She returns with DETECTIVE-INSPECTOR HILTON.

MRS LACEY: Mr Chance is out, sir, but we're expecting him
            back at any moment.

HILTON: (*Faintly annoyed*) But I received an urgent
            message that Mr Chance wanted to see me. I
            was under the impression …

MILLER: I sent the message, Inspector. (*To MRS LACEY*)
            It's all right, Mrs Lacey.

MRS LACEY goes into the kitchen.

HILTON: (*To MILLER*) What is this? What's it all about?

MILLER: I'm sorry if I interrupted your dinner, Inspector.

HILTON: Where is Chance?

MILLER: At the moment he's delivering a note to Miss
            Teckman.

HILTON: (*Puzzled*) Well?

MILLER: I had an appointment with him at a restaurant.
            When I arrived, he told me that he'd just had an
            interview with Martin Teckman.

HILTON: (*Astonished*) With Martin Teckman!

MILLER: Yes. Teckman apparently has asked him to
            deliver a note to his sister. Philip told me to get
            in touch with you and said he'd meet up back
            here.

HILTON: (*Incredulously*) But do you believe this story?
            Do you think he saw Teckman?

132

MILLER: (*Puzzled*) I don't know. I just can't make head or tail of it. I always thought Teckman was killed in the B.109.

HILTON: (*Thoughtfully*) So did I; so did a lot of other people. Did you see this man – the man he thought was Teckman?

MILLER: No, apparently he'd left just before I arrived.

HILTON: M'm. Well, we'd better wait and see what Chance has got to say about it.

A pause. HILTON looks at Miller, hesitates, then decides to speak.

HILTON: Mr Miller, I've been wanting to have a word with you, I nearly telephoned you yesterday morning.

MILLER: Well?

HILTON: I understand that you were in the R.A.F. with Martin Teckman – in the same Squadron, in fact.

MILLER: Yes, I told you that.

HILTON: Did you ever have any special buttons made, by any chance?

MILLER: (*Puzzled*) Buttons?

HILTON: Yes, with an R.A.F. inscription on them and the number of your Squadron?

MILLER: Oh, I see what you mean! Yes, I did, as a matter of fact I had them made for a blazer. Why do you ask?

HILTON: (*With a suggestion of a smile*) I wondered, that's all.

The sound of the front door opening and closing is heard.

MILLER: Yes, but you must have a reason for asking! You don't go around asking people whether they …

PHILIP enters.

PHILIP: (*To HILTON*) Oh, good! I was hoping you'd be here, Inspector! Has Maurice told you?

133

HILTON: He's told me that you're supposed to have seen Martin Teckman and that he …

PHILIP: There's no "supposed" about it! I did see Teckman. I spoke to him and he gave me a letter for his sister.

HILTON: Which I gather you've delivered?

PHILIP: Yes.

HILTON: Didn't it occur to you that that letter should have been taken straight to Scotland Yard?

PHILIP: (*Taken by surprise*) No, I'm afraid, I – I never thought of that.

A moment.

HILTON: Do you happen to know what was in the letter, Mr Chance?

PHILIP: Yes, Miss Teckman asked me to read it to her.

HILTON: Well?

PHILIP: (*Hesitates, then*) It was a farewell note. I got the impression that Teckman intended to either leave the country or …

HILTON: Or what?

PHILIP: Or commit suicide.

A pause. HILTON looks at PHILIP then suddenly his manner changes. He is more friendly.

HILTON: (*Humouring him*) Mr Chance, what makes you think this fellow was Martin Teckman? Oh, I know he said he was, and he gave you that letter, but that doesn't …

PHILIP: (*Adamant, on edge*) Inspector, there's no doubt about it! No shadow of doubt! I've seen photographs of Teckman, I recognised him. (*To MILLER*) I wish to goodness you'd turned up five minutes earlier, Maurice – you'd have recognised him, I feel sure.

HILTON looks at MILLER then back to PHILIP. His manner has changed again. He is still dubious but PHILIP's attitude has impressed him.

HILTON: (*Quietly; nodding*) You're convinced, aren't you, Mr Chance?

PHILIP: (*Emphatically*) It was Teckman.

HILTON: (*Resigned*) All right. (*He turns and picks up the telephone and commences to dial*) Well, this isn't going to be my baby! (*He stops dialling*) … (*On phone*) Hello? This is Detective-Inspector Hilton. Put me through to Major Harris, please.

CUT TO: The Lounge of RUTH WADE's flat.

DAVID JEFFERIES is sitting on the arm of an armchair reading a morning newspaper; he wears a light overcoat. He puts the newspaper down and calls to RUTH who is in one of the bedrooms.

JEFFERIES: It's nearly half past nine, Ruth!

RUTH: (*In the bedroom*) Coming, David!

JEFFERIES: (*Smiling; calling back*) It's a good job you don't have to work for a living!

RUTH comes out of the bedroom; she is dressed for business.

RUTH: I'll have you know it was half past ten when I left the office last night!

JEFFERIES: What on earth were you doing till half past ten?

RUTH: The great man's preparing a speech …

JEFFERIES: No! You surprise me!

The doorbell rings.

RUTH: I had to take the whole thing down in long hand.

JEFFERIES: That must have been jolly!

RUTH: Five thousand words – five hundred platitudes.

JEFFERIES: (*Laughing*) That's the front door, isn't it?

RUTH: Yes, I don't know who on earth it can be!

RUTH goes out to the front door. MAJOR HARRIS stands facing her.

HARRIS: Miss Wade?

RUTH: Yes.

HARRIS: Good morning, Miss Wade. My name is Major Harris. May I see you for a few moments, please?

RUTH: (*Hesitating*) Well –?

HARRIS: (*Smiling*) I'm not selling anything. Or collecting for charity.

RUTH still hesitates. DAVID JEFFERIES arrives at the door.

JEFFERIES: What is it, Ruth?

HARRIS: Mr Jefferies?

JEFFERIES: (*Puzzled*) Yes?

HARRIS: Good morning. I thought I recognised you. My name is Harris – Major Harris.

JEFFERIES: I'm sorry, I don't remember …

HARRIS: (*Interrupting*) I saw your wife last night, Mr Jefferies. We had a little chat.

JEFFERIES: (*Dubious*) My wife happens to be in hospital.

HARRIS: I know – St Matthews. She's in a private room on the third floor. (*Smiling*) You turn left as you get out of the lift; it's the third door on the right.

JEFFERIES: (*Irritated; a shade tense*) Who gave you permission to see my wife?

HARRIS: (*To RUTH*) May I come inside, Miss Wade? I assure you I'm not selling vacuum cleaners.

RUTH looks at JEFFERIES who hesitates then nods his head. HARRIS enters the lounge, followed by JEFFERIES and RUTH.

JEFFERIES: (*To HARRIS*) Now would you mind answering my question – who gave you permission to see my wife?

HARRIS: (*Quietly, to RUTH*) Is Mr Jefferies a friend of yours?

RUTH: He's my brother-in-law.

HARRIS: Oh, really? Barbara Jefferies is your sister then?

RUTH: Yes.

HARRIS: I didn't realise that. I must be slipping.

RUTH: Are you – from Scotland Yard?

HARRIS nods. JEFFERIES looks at RUTH then at HARRIS: he is puzzled.

HARRIS: I saw your wife, Mr Jefferies, because I wanted her to tell me, in her own words, precisely what happened the night she was knocked down.

JEFFERIES: (*Irritated*) My wife has already made two statements, one to Inspector Hilton and one …

HARRIS: (*Interrupting him; unperturbed*) Yes, I know, but I wanted to hear the story myself. (*To RUTH*) Miss Wade, I have certain questions I should like to ask you, but I think I ought to point out, in all fairness, that you are under no obligation to answer them.

RUTH: I'm prepared to answer any questions you like.

HARRIS: Thank you.

JEFFERIES: I think that's very unwise, Ruth. If I were you, I should say nothing and see your lawyer.

HARRIS: Would you, Mr Jefferies? That seems a little drastic.

JEFFERIES: I know you people. You twist things round to suit your own convenience.

HARRIS: Has that been your experience?

137

JEFFERIES:	I've never had anything to do with Scotland Yard.
HARRIS:	Then I suggest you don't know what you're talking about. (*Pleasantly; to RUTH*) Miss Wade, you strike me as being a rather sensible young lady, therefore I'm going to be perfectly frank with you. (*A moment*) You married Martin Teckman on June 3rd, 1952. You spent your honeymoon at a place called Mawnan Smith in Cornwall and you returned to London eight days later on June 11th. Is that correct?
RUTH:	(*Softly*) Yes …
HARRIS:	Now two days ago you telephoned a Mr Philip Chance and asked him to call round and see you.
RUTH:	Yes.
HARRIS:	Why? Why did you want to see Mr Chance?

RUTH glances at JEFFERIES.

RUTH:	(*After a moment's hesitation*) Well, as you probably know, my sister – Barbara Jefferies – intended to write a biography of my husband. Unfortunately, she had the accident and Philip Chance was asked to write the book instead.
HARRIS:	Go on …
RUTH:	(*Not too sure of herself*) Well, I thought that since Mr Chance was going to write about Martin it might be a very good idea if he met his wife. That's why I telephoned him.
HARRIS:	(*Watching RUTH*) I see. You had no other reason?
RUTH:	(*Undecided*) No, I – don't think so.

JEFFERIES: Look, Ruth – if you insist on answering his questions then for goodness sake answer them truthfully.

HARRIS: Thank you, Mr Jefferies.

JEFFERIES: (*To HARRIS*) Ruth was under the impression – call it a delusion, if you like – that her husband was still alive. She knew that Chance was a friend of Miss Teckman's and she wanted to know if Miss Teckman was of the same opinion.

HARRIS: Then why didn't she phone Miss Teckman instead of Chance?

RUTH: (*Coldly*) I'd never met Helen Teckman and I'd no wish to contact her.

HARRIS: Why not?

RUTH: (*Hesitating*) My husband was not very friendly with his sister and, well, it was just one of those things.

HARRIS: I see. (*Suddenly; quite pleasant*) Miss Wade, forgive my asking, but did you ever receive any letters from your husband?

RUTH: You mean, before we were married?

HARRIS: Before you were married, or afterwards, it makes no difference.

RUTH: (*Puzzled*) Why, yes, of course.

HARRIS: Do you happen to have one?

RUTH: Yes, I think so.

HARRIS: Could I see it?

RUTH looks at JEFFERIES then goes into the bedroom. There is a pause. JEFFERIES helps himself to a cigarette; flicks his lighter.

HARRIS: Was it a coincidence that your wife was asked to write a book about Teckman?

JEFFERIES: A coincidence?

HARRIS:	Or was it simply because she was Teckman's sister-in-law?
JEFFERIES:	I wouldn't know. That's obviously a question for Maurice Miller, the publisher.
HARRIS:	Well, here's a question for you. Do you share Miss Wade's opinion: do you think Teckman is alive?
JEFFERIES:	(*Thoughtfully; puzzled*) When the suggestion was first made, I thought the whole idea was ridiculous – too fantastic for words. Now – (*A shrug*) I just don't know.
HARRIS:	You know, of course, that Sir Charles Shaughnessy was supposed to have seen Teckman?
JEFFERIES:	Yes, Ruth told me.
HARRIS:	You think he was mistaken?
JEFFERIES:	I wouldn't like to say whether he was mistaken or not. There's something very funny about the whole business. If Teckman is alive then why hasn't he been in touch with Shaughnessy?
HARRIS:	Why, indeed?
JEFFERIES:	And why hasn't he contacted Ruth? It just doesn't make sense. They were devoted to each other.
HARRIS:	(*Watching JEFFERIES*) Were they, Mr Jefferies?

RUTH returns from the bedroom; she is holding a sheet of notepaper.

RUTH:	(*Handing HARRIS the letter*) Here's a note I received from Martin about a week after we were married. It's not very personal – you can keep it if you want to.
HARRIS:	Thank you.

HARRIS looks at the letter.

HARRIS: I'll let you have this back, Miss Wade.
RUTH: Yes, all right.
HARRIS looks at the letter again; there is a long pause. RUTH looks across at JEFFERIES. HARRIS slowly looks up.
HARRIS: (*To JEFFERIES*) I'm glad your wife is getting better, Mr Jefferies.
JEFFERIES: Yes, it's a great relief.
HARRIS: (*Looking at JEFFERIES and nodding*) I'm sure it   must be.
HARRIS looks at the letter again; it is difficult to tell whether his mind is on Barbara Jefferies or the letter.

CUT TO: The Drawing Room of PHILIP's flat.
PHILIP and DETECTIVE-INSPECTOR HILTON are facing each other. PHILIP looks faintly irritated.
PHILIP: I'm afraid I don't see what you're getting at, Inspector.
HILTON: I'm not getting at anything, sir. I'm simply asking you a perfectly simple question. Did Mr Miller ever stay here – in the flat?
PHILIP: No.
HILTON: You're quite sure?
PHILIP: Yes, I'm quite – (*Stops*) Oh, wait a minute! He stayed here one night, about six weeks ago …
HELTON: Why was that?
PHILIP: They were redecorating his place; it was in a frightful mess, so I said he could stay here the night.
HILTON: I see. Was that a weekend?
PHILIP: It was a Saturday. I remember it very well because we played golf in the afternoon and I beat him. (*Smiling*) A most unusual procedure.
HILTON: (*Pleasantly*) Thank you, Mr Chance. You've been very helpful.

PHILIP: I'm glad to hear it.

We now see that MAJOR HARRIS has been sitting in an armchair listening to this conversation.

HARRIS: Mr Chance, when are you seeing Miss Teckman again?

PHILIP: Tonight. I'm taking her out to dinner.

HARRIS: (*Smiling*) Have you got any influence with her?

PHILIP: A little, I imagine.

HARRIS: (*Quietly; taking RUTH's note out of his wallet*) I wonder if you'd give her a piece of advice?

PHILIP: Well – what is it?

HARRIS: Advise her not to see Miss Wade, not yet at any rate.

PHILIP: What makes you think she wants to?

HARRIS: According to what you've told us she's just discovered that Ruth Wade's her sister-in-law, so naturally she'll want to meet Miss Wade.

PHILIP: And you don't want her to?

HARRIS: I think it would be a little unwise, just at the moment.

PHILIP: All right, I'll tell her.

HARRIS: (*Smiling*) No, I don't want you to tell her, I want you to advise her. If you tell her not to see Miss Wade, ten to one she'll make a point of seeing her – you know what women are.

PHILIP: Yes, I know – but I'm rather surprised to find you do, Major.

The INSPECTOR smiles.

HARRIS: (*Unperturbed*) Life's full of surprises.

HARRIS rises.

HILTON: Mr Chance, before we go, there's just one point Major Harris and I would like to get quite clear. You say the man in the restaurant – we'll call him Teckman for the time being …

PHILIP: It was Teckman!

HILTON: All right, Teckman. You say, he gave you a letter for his sister, a letter which you eventually delivered.

PHILIP: Yes.

HILTON: Now what actually happened to that letter before you delivered it to Miss Teckman?

PHILIP: I don't understand?

HILTON: Well, we know for instance that you were called to the telephone, that's when Teckman made his get-a-way …

PHILIP: Yes.

HILTON: Did you take the letter with you into the telephone box?

PHILIP: No, it was left on the table.

HILTON: And you picked it up later?

PHILIP: Yes.

HILTON: Immediately you came out of the phone box?

PHILIP: No, immediately I came out of the box I saw that Teckman had disappeared and I – well, I went after him.

HILTON: That's when you bumped into Miller?

PHILIP: Yes. I dashed out into the street, there was no sign of Teckman, so I went back into the restaurant to see Miller.

HILTON: And it was then that you picked up the letter?

PHILIP: Yes.

HILTON: It was still on the table?

PHILIP: Yes, of course it was!

HARRIS: (*Passing PHILIP Ruth's note*) Mr Chance, I want you to have a look at this note.

PHILIP takes the note and looks at it. A pause.

PHILIP: (*Looking up*) Well?

HARRIS: Would you say that that note had been written by the same person that wrote the letter?

PHILIP: I most certainly wouldn't, the handwriting is quite different!

HARRIS: (*Taking the note out of PHILIP's hand*) Thank you, Mr Chance. That's what I wanted to know.

CUT TO: The front door of HELEN's flat.

HELEN arrives with PHILIP. They have been dining together. It is night. HELEN takes a key out of her handbag.

PHILIP: I'll say good night.

HELEN: Wouldn't you like to come in for a drink?

PHILIP: No, I don't think I will, it's getting rather late.

HELEN: (*Smiling*) It must be at least ten o'clock.

PHILIP: (*Laughing*) Yes.

HELEN: (*Holding out her hand*) Well – thank you for a very nice dinner.

PHILIP: (*Taking HELEN's hand*) Try not to worry too much.

HELEN: I'm afraid I've been rather dull company this evening.

PHILIP: No, of course you haven't.

HELEN: Are you sure you wouldn't like a drink?

PHILIP: I'm sure I – (*Changes his mind*) would like one.

HELEN: (*Laughing*) Come along! I knew you'd change your mind!

HELEN turns towards the door and puts the key in the lock.

CUT TO: The Drawing Room of HELEN's flat.

HELEN enters followed by PHILIP.

HELEN: (*Crossing towards the bedroom*) I shan't be a moment, Philip!

PHILIP: Yes, all right.

HELEN: (*Indicating the drinks on a nearby table*) Take your things off and help yourself to a drink.

144

PHILIP: Would you like something?

HELEN: No, I don't think so. Yes, I'll have a spot of brandy.

PHILIP: Now who's changing their mind!

HELEN laughs and goes into the bedroom. PHILIP takes off his coat; crosses to the table and mixes the drinks. After a little while HELEN comes out of the bedroom; she looks puzzled; thoughtful. PHILIP turns towards her with the brandy.

PHILIP: Here we are. (*He stops*) What is it?

HELEN: (*Looking up; quietly*) Philip, someone's been in the flat.

PHILIP: What makes you think so?

HELEN: The place has been searched. They've been in my bedroom …

PHILIP puts the glass down and quickly crosses into the bedroom. HELEN stares round the room; obviously puzzled and worried. PHILIP returns.

PHILIP: (*Puzzled*) Helen, are you sure? Everything looks all right …

HELEN: I'm positive.

PHILIP: Well – haven't you got a maid?

HELEN: (*Tense; still looking round the room*) Yes, but she doesn't live in – in any case she's away at the moment.

PHILIP: (*Crossing towards HELEN*) You know, I think you're imagining things.

HELEN: (*Tensely*) No, I'm not. Someone's been here. I know it. I can feel it.

PHILIP: (*Taking HELEN by the arm*) Now look, my dear – you're terribly overwrought … You've got to take things easy …

HELEN: Philip, why should anyone want to search my flat?

PHILIP: I don't know why – Now look, Helen – you know what I told you earlier this evening?

145

HELEN: About – not seeing Ruth Wade?

PHILIP: (*Shaking his head*) No, no, about going away for two or three weeks.

HELEN: I can't, Philip. Not now …

PHILIP: Why not?

HELEN: Supposing Martin wants to see me?

PHILIP: If Martin had wanted to see you, he'd have seen you a long time ago. (*Holding HELEN's arm tight*) There's something you've got to realise, and the sooner you realise it the better. I know Martin's your brother, I know you're desperately fond of him, but you're driving yourself into a first-class nervous breakdown over a man who isn't worth … Helen, you're not listening to me!

HELEN: (*She hasn't heard PHILIP; her manner is tense*) Do you think Ruth Wade's been here? Do you think   it was …

PHILIP: (*A shade annoyed*) I don't think anyone has been here! Helen, for goodness sake! What makes you think the flat's been searched?

HELEN: (*Quickly; looking at PHILIP*) I've got two silver brushes; they're identical to look at but one of them has a small dent.

The telephone starts ringing.

HELEN: Now I always keep the brushes side by side but the one with the dent … (*She stops and looks at the telephone*)

PHILIP: Shall I take it?

HELEN: (*A pause; softly*) No, it's all right …

HELEN crosses and picks up the telephone. A slight pause.

HELEN: (*On the phone*) Hello? … Yes, speaking … (*Suddenly*) Martin! Martin, where are you? … Yes, darling, I'm listening … (*Quickly*) Where? … Yes, of course I will … Yes, of course …

146

(*Desperately*) Martin, don't ring off! Not yet … not yet, please, darling! (*She looks at the receiver; the line is dead*)

PHILIP crosses and quickly takes the phone from HELEN.

PHILIP: What happened? What did he say?

HELEN: He wants to see me! He wants to see me tomorrow night!

PHILIP: Where?

HELEN: He said – Auberge d'Armaille. Is that the restaurant where you saw him before?

PHILIP: Yes. What time?

HELEN: Ten o'clock. Oh, Philip! I knew he'd ring … I knew he'd want to see me.

PHILIP: (*Putting down the telephone*) Yes, well, this is one appointment you don't keep, Miss Teckman!

HELEN: (*Stunned*) What do you mean? Philip, I've got to see him! Whatever happens I've got to see him.

PHILIP: You'll see him all right. (*PHILIP puts his hands on HELEN's shoulders and looks into her face*) But you're not keeping that appointment.

CUT TO: The Auberge d'Armaille Restaurant.

The MAN (MARTIN TECKMAN) is sitting at a table in the restaurant reading the menu. It is the corner table facing the window, back to the wall. He puts down the menu and glances at his watch; takes out his cigarette case, is about to extract a cigarette when he notices someone enter the restaurant. He is obviously surprised; replaces the cigarette case and slowly rises from the table. PHILIP is in the restaurant entrance. He sees TECKMAN and crosses to the table.

MAN: (*Quickly; surprised*) What are you doing here? Where's Helen?

PHILIP: (*Quietly*) Helen's not coming!

MAN: What do you mean – she's not coming? Did you give her my letter?

PHILIP: Yes, of course I did.

MAN: (*Tensely*) Well – what are you doing here? What is it you want?

PHILIP: (*Quietly*) It's all over, Teckman.

MAN: You mean –?

PHILIP: (*Nodding*) Inspector Hilton's here and Major Harris.

MAN: Harris?

PHILIP: He's with M.I.5.

MAN: Does Helen know that you've sent for the police?

From the street outside there is the sound of an approaching car; it is being driven very fast.

PHILIP: I didn't exactly send for them; in any case don't worry about Helen because …

The MAN makes a quick movement away from the table, but PHILIP restrains him.

PHILIP: It's no good trying to make a dash for it. The place is surrounded. Teckman, it's no use! Don't be a fool!

MAN: (*A moment*) Yes, all right.

PHILIP: Have you got a coat?

MAN: (*Nodding*) It's in the cloakroom.

As TECKMAN speaks there is the sound of machine gun fire from the car; the smashing of the restaurant window. PHILIP dives for TECKMAN and drags him to the floor. The wall behind the table is sprayed with machine gun bullets.

END OF EPISODE FIVE

EPISODE SIX

THIRD PERSON SINGULAR

OPEN TO: The table in the restaurant

PHILIP and the MAN (TECKMAN) are on the floor; the windows are smashed; the wall sprayed with bullets. We can hear noises and excited voices from both inside and outside the restaurant. PHILIP slowly raises himself; turns and looks at the still figure of MARTIN TECKMAN. PHILIP is dazed and confused. He crosses to TECKMAN as DETECTIVE-INSPECTOR HILTON and MAJOR HARRIS dash into view. HILTON gives his attention to PHILIP while HARRIS kneels down and examines TECKMAN.

HILTON: (*To PHILIP*) Are you hurt?

PHILIP: No ... No, they missed me. I don't know about Teckman.

HILTON looks across at HARRIS.

HARRIS: (*Looking up*) It's Teckman all right. Get an ambulance here as quickly as you can.

They all look towards TECKMAN.

CUT TO: The Drawing Room of PHILIP's flat.

HELEN TECKMAN is walking up and down the room; obviously waiting for PHILIP; she is tense and on edge. MRS LACEY comes out of the kitchen; she is dressed for going home and carries a shopping basket.

MRS LACEY: I'll be trotting now, Miss, if you don't mind.

HELEN: Yes, you run along, Mrs Lacey.

MRS LACEY: I didn't think Mr Chance would be as late as this!

HELEN: No, neither did I.

MRS LACEY: It's 'alf past eleven. My hubby'll wonder what's 'appened to me. (*Suddenly; indicating her basket*) Oh, you might tell Mr Chance I've taken some of the baking power.

HELEN: (*Her thoughts elsewhere*) Yes, all right, Mrs Lacey.

MRS LACEY goes out as the telephone starts to ring. HELEN quickly picks up the receiver.

HELEN: (*On phone*) Hello? … Hello? …

CUT TO: *MAURICE MILLER, wearing a dressing-gown, holding his telephone receiver.*

MILLER: Can I speak to Mr Chance, please?

HELEN: (*On the other end of the phone*) I'm sorry, he's not in …

MILLER: (*After giving the phone a significant look; surprised to hear a girl's voice*) Oh – well – are you expecting him?

HELEN: Yes, he should be here at any moment.

MILLER: Well, would you be kind enough to deliver a message?

HELEN: Yes, certainly.

MILLER: Tell him I'll call round and see him tomorrow morning – about half past eleven.

HELEN: What name shall I say?

MILLER: Miller – Maurice Miller.

HELEN: Yes, all right, Mr Miller, I'll deliver your message.

MILLER: Thank you. (*He looks at the receiver before replacing it. He is curious about HELEN's presence in PHILIP's flat*)

CUT TO: The Drawing Room of PHILIP's flat.
HELEN replaces the telephone receiver. She suddenly looks up having heard the sound of the front door opening and closing. PHILIP enters. He looks tired and very serious.

PHILIP: Was that the telephone?

HELEN: Yes, it was Maurice Miller. He wants to see you. He's calling round tomorrow morning.

152

	(*Tensely*) Philip, what happened? Did you see Martin?
PHILIP:	Yes, I saw him.
HELEN:	(*Quickly*) Well – what happened? (*A moment*) What is it? What's the matter?
PHILIP:	Helen, do you mind if I have a drink first, I …

PHILIP crosses to the drinks on the table.

HELEN:	No, of course not. (*Watching PHILIP: puzzled*) Are you all right?
PHILIP:	(*Mixing himself a drink*) Yes, but I've had a rather nasty experience, Helen. I'll – I'll be all right when I've had a drink.

PHILIP drinks and then replaces the glass on the table. He turns towards HELEN and faces her.

PHILIP:	I saw your brother. He was going to give himself up and then …
HELEN:	Philip, tell me! What happened?
PHILIP:	A car drove past the restaurant. They fired through the restaurant. Your brother was hit …
HELEN:	Oh …
PHILIP:	(*Taking holds of HELEN's arm*) I'm sorry, Helen. He's dead …

HELEN lowers her head. PHILIP grips her arm.

CUT TO: The Lounge of RUTH WADE's flat.

DAVID JEFFERIES is sitting on the arm of a chair glancing through the pages of a magazine. He looks up and calls to RUTH who is in the bedroom.

JEFFERIES:	Why don't you try getting up half an hour earlier!
RUTH:	(*From the bedroom*) I did – and I didn't like it!

RUTH enters.

RUTH:	Sorry, David! I always seem to keep you waiting, don't I?

153

JEFFERIES:	It wouldn't be so bad if you got a new magazine once in a while!

RUTH laughs.

RUTH:	Are we going to be late?
JEFFERIES:	No, we've got plenty of time. We don't want to get to the hospital too early; the Day Sister's a bit on the difficult side.
RUTH:	Well, you seem to have won her over.
JEFFERIES:	(*Shaking his head*) It's Barbara – she's really gone to Town on her!
RUTH:	(*Smiling*) I'm awfully glad Barbara's getting better, David.
JEFFERIES:	It's a relief I can tell you!
RUTH:	I wonder if they'll ever find the person who did it?
JEFFERIES:	You mean the driver of the car?
RUTH:	Yes.
JEFFERIES:	I doubt it. And curiously enough, I shall be rather relieved if they don't.
RUTH:	Yes, I suppose if they find him there'll be a case and Barbara will have to be a witness and all that nonsense.
JEFFERIES:	Exactly. I'd like to get Barbara away for two or three weeks – into the country somewhere.
RUTH:	Well, there's always my cottage.
JEFFERIES:	You're very sweet, Ruth.

The doorbell rings.

JEFFERIES:	As a matter of fact, you've been awfully kind over this business. I haven't had a chance of thanking you.
RUTH:	Nonsense! I'm very fond of Barbara, you know that. (*Crossing to the front door*) Excuse me – that's probably the paper boy!

CUT TO: *RUTH opening the front door. The visitor is MAJOR HARRIS*.

HARRIS: Good morning, Miss Wade!

RUTH: (*Surprised*) Oh, good morning!

HARRIS: (*Pleasantly*) May I come in?

RUTH: Yes, of course.

CUT back to the lounge.

MAJOR HARRIS enters followed by RUTH.

HARRIS: (*On seeing JEFFERIES*) Oh, good morning, Mr Jefferies! I didn't expect to find you here!

JEFFERIES: I'm taking Miss Wade to the hospital: we're going to see my wife.

HARRIS: And how is Mrs Jefferies?

JEFFERIES: She's very much better, thank you.

HARRIS: I'm delighted to hear it.

RUTH: With a bit of luck, she'll be home by the end of next week.

HARRIS: Oh, splendid. (*To JEFFERIES*) It must be quite a relief.

JEFFERIES: It is, I can assure you.

HARRIS: (*After a moment; pleasantly*) Mr Jefferies, someone told me the other day, rather to my surprise, that you used to be on the stage?

JEFFERIES: I did.

HARRIS: That's interesting. What did you do, exactly?

JEFFERIES: Oh, straight plays, revues – pretty well everything.

HARRIS: Why did you give it up?

JEFFERIES: My father died and I – went into the family business.

HARRIS: I see.

JEFFERIES: We deal in stationery – wholesale – in case you're interested.

HARRIS smiles, takes a note out of his pocket and turns towards RUTH.

HARRIS: I brought you your note back, Miss Wade.

RUTH: (*Taking the note*) Oh, thank you, I hope it was helpful.

HARRIS: It was indeed. (*He consults his watch*) What time are you due at St Matthews?

JEFFERIES: About half past ten.

HARRIS: (*Nods. To RUTH*) I suggest that while Mr Jefferies is talking to his wife you have a word with the House Surgeon. Tell him I've given you permission to see the patient in 204.

JEFFERIES: (*Puzzled*) The patient in 204?

HARRIS: Yes.

JEFFERIES looks at RUTH.

RUTH: But why should I want to see the patient in 204?

HARRIS: (*After a moment*) He's your husband …

CUT TO: The Drawing Room of PHILIP's flat.

PHILIP is at his desk writing a letter. The doorbell is ringing, and MRS LACEY comes out of the kitchen and crosses towards the door.

PHILIP: That's probably Mr Miller – if it is, ask him in.

MRS LACEY: Yes, sir.

PHILIP finishes his letter as MRS LACEY returns with MAURICE MILLER.

MRSLACEY: Mr Miller, sir.

PHILIP: (*Rising*) Hello, Maurice!

MRS LACEY goes into the kitchen.

MILLER: Good morning, Philip. I trust I'm not disturbing a creative impulse.

PHILIP: I was writing a letter, that's all.

MILLER: You surprise me.

156

PHILIP:	Not so much of the heavy sarcasm. Let me take your things.
MILLER:	No, I can't stay. I only dropped in to have a word with you. Philip, when I was here the other day that detective fellow, what was his name –?
PHILIP:	Hilton.
MILLER:	That's it, Hilton! Well, he asked me a very peculiar question. I've been worried about it.
PHILIP:	Well, I shouldn't worry about it – he's been asking me peculiar questions for days.
MILLER:	Yes, but this did worry me. You see, he happens to be right.
PHILIP:	What about?
MILLER:	About the button.
PHILIP:	The button?
MILLER:	Yes.
PHILIP:	Supposing we talk in Hindustani, then neither of us will know what it's all about?
MILLER:	No, you don't understand, old boy. He asked me if I'd ever had any buttons engraved with RAF insignia and my Squadron number.
PHILIP:	Well?
MILLER:	Well, I told him that I had.
PHILIP:	(*Surprised*) But what on earth did you do that for?
MILLER:	Because it's true! I did have some special buttons made. They were made for a blazer. You know, the blue one – you've seen me wear it.
PHILIP:	Yes, I believe I have now you come to mention it.

MILLER: Well, to cut a long story short, I've lost a button and I'm wondering if – well, if that's what he was getting at.

PHILIP: That's what he was getting at all right!

MILLER: Well – what's the point?

PHILIP: They found your button here – in the flat – the morning after the robbery.

MILLER: Did they, by Jove! Then that explains it!

PHILIP: Yes.

MILLER: I must have lost it when I stayed here – the weekend we played golf. Do you remember?

PHILIP: The day I won.

MILLER: That's – (*Laughing*) Yes, that's right. (*Suddenly*) I say, look here, Philip, they don't think that button's a frightfully important clue and I had something to do with the robbery?

PHILIP: No, I don't think so, but the button puzzled them because both you and Teckman happened to be in the same Squadron.

MILLER: By George, yes! Now I understand why that fellow Harris was so interested in me. But who actually broke into your flat, do you know?

PHILIP: Yes, curiously enough they picked him up this morning. He was a jewel thief; one of the regulars.

MILLER: Well, why on earth did he ransack the place?

PHILIP: He was looking for jewellery. He thought this was the flat above – Lady Delaford's.

MILLER: Oh, I see.

PHILIP: Would you like a drink, Maurice?

MILLER: No, thanks, old boy. It's too early for me – in any case, I must be making a move. (*A moment: almost casually:*) Philip, what happened about Teckman? Is there any news?

PHILIP: Yes.

158

MILLER: Well?

PHILIP: (*Hesitant*) I'll – I'll tell you all about it some other time, Maurice.

MILLER: Yes, all right, old man.

MILLER looks at PHILIP, obviously very curious.

PHILIP: By the way, I understand Barbara Jefferies is very much better.

MILLER: Yes, there's been a great improvement. There's some talk of her coming out of the hospital next week.

PHILIP: Oh, really? Who told you that?

MILLER: Her husband. I bumped into him last night in the Club.

PHILIP: Oh, I see. (*Thoughtfully*) He's a curious bird.

MILLER: Yes.

PHILIP: What does he do exactly?

The telephone starts to ring.

MILLER: Haven't the slightest idea. Still Barbara does frightfully well, you know. Her books sell like hot cakes. Well, I must be off!

PHILIP: (*Crossing to the phone*) Excuse me, Maurice!

MILLER: I'll let myself out.

PHILIP: (*Picking up the phone*) Yes, all right. I'll probably phone you tomorrow. We'll fix a lunch date.

MILLER: Right!

MILLER gives a little wave to PHILIP and goes out.

PHILIP: (*On phone*) Hello?

HELEN: (*On the other end*) Philip?

PHILIP: Oh, hello, Helen!

CUT TO: *HELEN on telephone in her flat.*

HELEN: I understand you've been trying to get me?

PHILIP: Yes, I phoned you this morning, but you were out. Helen, there's something I want to ask you.

159

HELEN: Yes?

CUT TO   PHILIP

PHILIP: No, I can't ask you on the phone, I – look, are you doing anything this afternoon?

HELEN: No. I had an appointment at the hairdressers, but I've cancelled it.

PHILIP: Well, come and have some tea with me. About four o'clock.

CUT TO HELEN

HELEN: Yes, all right. (*A moment*) What is this question, Philip? Is it important?

PHILIP: I think so.

HELEN: To – me?

PHILIP: To both of us, Helen. Four o'clock?

HELEN: Yes, all right, dear.

CUT TO PHILIP

PHILIP replaces the receiver. We now see that MAJOR HARRIS and DETECTIVE-INSPECTOR HILTON have entered the room and are standing watching PHILIP.

HILTON: We saw Miller – he left the door open for us.

PHILIP: That's all right, Inspector! Come in!

HILTON: Thank you, sir.

PHILIP: (*To HARRIS*) Good morning, Major.

HARRIS: Good morning!

HILTON: Did you get my message?

PHILIP: About the robbery?

HILTON: Yes.

PHILIP: (*Nodding*) The Sergeant telephoned. Are you sure you've got the right man?

HILTON: (*Nodding*) He's admitted it.

HARRIS: Mr Chance, I came round this morning because I feel I owe you an apology.

PHILIP: (*Faintly surprised*) Indeed?

HARRIS: May I sit down?

PHILIP: Yes, of course! I'm sorry, Inspector?

HILTON: Thank you, sir.

The INSPECTOR and MAJOR HARRIS sit in the armchairs. PHILIP stands by his desk.

PHILIP: You were saying, Major?

HARRIS: When this Teckman business first started I was under the impression that you were mixed up in it.

PHILIP: But I am mixed up in it!

HARRIS: (*Smiling*) Yes, but in rather a different way from what I suspected.

PHILIP: What did you suspect?

HILTON: In order to answer that, sir, we should have to take you into our confidence.

PHILIP: Well, why don't you? It would make a nice change.

HARRIS looks at HILTON.

HARRIS: Mr Chance, during the past two or three days you've been both helpful and co-operative. We appreciate it.

PHILIP: But not enough to take me into your confidence?

HARRIS: Unfortunately, we can't – for security reasons.

PHILIP: Good old security!

HARRIS: But nevertheless, there are certain facts which I think you ought to know about.

PHILIP: Well?

HARRIS: Teckman was a member of a certain political group. The head of that group – shall we say X? – persuaded, or possibly blackmailed, Teckman into flying the B.109 to a secret base. Well – we know what happened. Teckman changed his mind;

161

crashed the plane and baled out. Now so far as the group were concerned this was a very serious situation. Not only had Teckman double-crossed them over the B.109, but he was in the unique position of knowing every important member of the group. Teckman, therefore, had to be eliminated.

PHILIP: Go on …

HARRIS: Now when Barbara Jefferies started making inquiries about Teckman, in order to get material for the biography, the group realised that she might inadvertently discover that Teckman had been interested in politics and was in fact one of their ex-members. Her investigations had to be stopped, only as a precautionary measure.

HILTON: But the moment Barbara Jefferies stopped making inquiries, you appeared on the scene. Now obviously you couldn't be the victim of a motor car accident – that would be too big a coincidence – so they decided to make you a proposition, the sort of proposition you just couldn't refuse.

PHILIP: You mean they wanted to get me out of the way, so they sent me – or tried to send me – to Berlin?

HARRIS: Yes.

HILTON: What would have happened in Berlin we leave to your imagination.

PHILIP: But what about the letter of introduction?

HARRIS: Well, the letter of introduction was an interesting development and was, curiously enough, partly responsible for our discovering the identity of X. When Rice, who was of course a member of the group, realised that you had fallen for the Berlin proposition, he saw no reason why you shouldn't take a personal message to Rudolph Kesner.

162

HILTON: Kesner is the head of the whole outfit and he'd given specific instructions to the group that Teckman had to be found.

PHILIP: But the letter of introduction was simply a drawing of the B.109.

HARRIS: (*Smiling*) You think so, Mr Chance?

PHILIP: Well – wasn't it?

HARRIS: (*Shaking his head*) No …

PHILIP: Well – what was in the letter?

A pause. HILTON looks at HARRIS. PHILIP notices the look.

PHILIP: Now look here, Major Harris. I've got a hunch about this business and I'm going to play it.

HILTON: What do you mean, sir?

PHILIP: You came here this afternoon because you want me to do something for you; if you didn't you wouldn't have told me as much as you have done. Now I'm prepared to help you; I'm prepared to do anything you want, providing you take me into your confidence. If you don't – I shan't even raise my little finger.

HARRIS: (*Quietly; serious*) Have you got any idea what it is we want you to do, Mr Chance?

PHILIP: (*A moment; seriously*) Yes, I have.

HARRIS: (*After a moment*) All right. (*Nodding*) Cards on the table.

PHILIP: Well, you can start by telling me about Andrew Garvin. Who murdered Garvin and why was he found in my flat?

HARRIS: Garvin was murdered by Rice and for obvious reasons. He knew too much about Teckman – and what he didn't know he suspected.

PHILIP: Yes, but why pick that particular moment to murder him? After all, Rice must have known for a very long time that Garvin was a friend of Teckman's,

163

everyone else knew it. Everyone knew about Garvin's theory.

HILTON: Yes, and everyone thought that the theory, like Garvin himself, was something of a joke. But then suddenly, things began to happen. Certain people began to think that perhaps Teckman wasn't dead, in which case Garvin's theory wasn't quite so far-fetched after all.

PHILIP: Yes, I can see now why they murdered him – but why bring him to my flat?

HILTON: (*Smiling*) Don't you know why, Mr Chance?

PHILIP: You mean – to throw suspicion on to me?

HILTON: No. What was your immediate reaction when you discovered Garvin?

PHILIP: I was horrified …

HILTON: Yes, I know, but –

PHILIP: I was also a little frightened; I thought you might think that I'd murdered him.

HILTON: And when you found out that we didn't think you murdered him?

PHILIP: I wanted to forget the whole business; Garvin; the biography; everything to do with Teckman.

HARRIS: In other words, you couldn't get to Berlin quick enough.

HILTON: Exactly!

PHILIP: Yes, I see what you mean!

HARRIS: Chance, a moment ago you asked me about the letter of introduction, and I told you that it wasn't just a drawing of the B.109. The drawing simply proved to Kesner that it was a genuine message from Rice. The message itself was in invisible ink and stated that …

HILTON: … In Rice's opinion X wasn't fully co-operating in the attempt to find Teckman.

164

HARRIS:	In other words, Rice wanted to take over from X and become head of the group. X discovered what Rice was up to and – well, you know what happened to him.
PHILIP:	I see.
HARRIS:	(*Quietly; looking at PHILIP*) We don't have to tell you who X is – do we, Mr Chance?
PHILIP:	(*Shaking his head*) No – you don't have to tell me.

CUT TO: The Storey Club

DAVID JEFFERIES arrives wearing outdoor clothes and is just about to go into the telephone box when MAURICE MILLER arrives. JEFFERIES hesitates.

MILLER:	Hello, Jefferies!
JEFFERIES:	Oh, hello, Miller!
MILLER:	Have you seen Barbara today?
JEFFERIES:	Yes, I saw her this morning. There's a great deal of improvement. She's coming out of hospital next week.
MILLER:	Oh, splendid! Well, we've got rather a nice surprise for her. We're bringing out a collected edition of her novels.
JEFFERIES:	Are you, by Jove? That'll please her.
MILLER:	I suppose it'll be a long time before she gets down to work again?
JEFFERIES:	I don't know. She was talking about it this morning. I shouldn't be surprised if she doesn't start writing again in a month or two.
MILLER:	Really? That's jolly good. Would she be interested in the biography, do you think?
JEFFERIES:	You mean the Teckman biography?
MILLER:	Yes.

JEFFERIES: I thought you'd asked Philip Chance to write it?

MILLER: I did. I've got a contract with him as a matter of fact, but –

JEFFERIES: But what?

MILLER: Well, Barbara was our first choice. I feel quite sure that Philip would step down if she's still interested.

JEFFERIES: I'll have a word with her about it.

MILLER: Yes, all right.

JEFFERIES: If you'll excuse me – I want to make a phone call.

MILLER: Yes, of course. Goodbye, old man.

JEFFERIES: Goodbye.

JEFFERIES looks after MILLER, then enters the telephone box.

CUT TO: The interior of the telephone box.

JEFFERIES lifts the receiver; puts money into the box and dials. His manner is a shade apprehensive; he glances through either side of the glass, as if he does not wish to be seen telephoning.

We hear the number ringing out.

CUT TO: The Drawing Room of HELEN TECKMAN's flat.

The telephone is ringing. HELEN answers it. For the duration of this conversation, we cut back and forth between HELEN and JEFFERIES.

HELEN: (*On phone*) Hello? …

JEFFERIES presses button 'A'

HELEN: Hello?

JEFFERIES: (*Quietly*) Is that you Helen?

HELEN: (*Puzzled*) Who is that?

JEFFERIES: Don't you recognise my voice?

HELEN: (*Still puzzled*) No, I'm afraid I don't …
JEFFERIES: You should, Helen.
HELEN: Why? Who are you?

JEFFERIES leans towards the mouthpiece and commences to whistle "Charmaine". HELEN stares at her receiver with astonishment; she looks bewildered.

CUT TO: The Drawing Room of PHILIP's flat.

PHILIP is sitting in an armchair glancing through the pages of a book. MRS LACEY comes out of the kitchen wheeling a tea trolley. She is wearing a hat and her outdoor clothes.

MRS LACEY: Here's your tea, sir.

PHILIP: Oh, thank you, Mrs Lacey.

MRS LACEY: You're sure there's nothing else?

PHILIP: No, that's fine. You can go now.

The doorbell rings.

MRS LACEY: I've spoken to the laundry, sir – everything's all right.

PHILIP: Thank you, Mrs Lacey. (*Nodding towards the alcove*) I think that's Miss Teckman – ask her in, will you?

MRS LACEY: Yes, certainly, sir.

MRS LACEY goes out. PHILIP stands looking towards the alcove. MRS LACEY returns with HELEN.

PHILIP: Hello, Helen! It's nice to see you. Come in!

MRS LACEY: I'll be off now, sir.

PHILIP: Yes, goodbye, Mrs Lacey.

MRS LACEY: (*To HELEN*) Good afternoon, miss.

HELEN: (*Hardly taking any notice of MRS LACEY*) Goodbye …

MRS LACEY goes out.

PHILIP: (*Crossing towards HELEN*) Helen, you look very strange. Has something happened?

HELEN: (*Tensely*) Why did you lie to me?

167

PHILIP:	Lie to you?
HELEN:	You told me Martin was dead …
PHILIP:	Well?
HELEN:	(*Tensely*) He's not. He's not dead – he telephoned me half an hour ago.
PHILIP:	Martin did?
HELEN:	Yes.
PHILIP:	(*Shaking his head*) You're mistaken … You must be mistaken because …
HELEN:	I'm not mistaken, Philip. It was Martin.
PHILIP:	Did he say so?
HELEN:	No, he didn't actually say so, but –
PHILIP:	You recognised his voice?
HELEN:	Yes. (*Hesitant*) Yes, I think I did. It sounded like Martin, and yet …
PHILIP:	You're not sure.
HELEN:	He whistled that tune again – "Charmaine".
PHILIP:	Well, that's doesn't prove anything, does it? I could have telephoned you and whistled "Charmaine". (*He takes HELEN by the arm*) Look, Helen, this business has been a terrible strain for you. I do advise you …
HELEN:	Philip, please! If it wasn't Martin, then who was it?
A pause.	
PHILIP:	(*Facing HELEN; deliberately*) It wasn't Martin, Helen.
HELEN:	You're sure?
PHILIP:	(*Nodding*) I'm absolutely sure.
HELEN:	(*Turning away*) Then who was it? And why should anyone want to do a thing like that?
PHILIP:	(*Quietly*) Don't you know why?
HELEN:	(*Turning towards PHILIP again*) No – no, I don't – do you?

168

A pause.

PHILIP: (*Quietly*) Let me get you some tea.

HELEN: (*Facing him*) Philip, answer my question! If it wasn't Martin – then who was it?

PHILIP looks at HELEN; his manner is quiet; strangely enigmatic.

PHILIP: Let me get you some tea, Helen.

PHILIP pours out two cups of tea; adds milk.

PHILIP: Do you take sugar?

HELEN: (*Strained; looking at him; puzzled*) It doesn't matter.

PHILIP: (*Handing HELEN a cup of tea*) Here we are, Helen.

The telephone starts to ring.

HELEN: Philip, you haven't answered my question. If it wasn't … (*She hesitates and looks across at the telephone*)

PHILIP: Excuse me.

PHILIP crosses to the telephone; his back to HELEN who is watching him intently. Suddenly she opens her handbag and – with her eyes still on PHILIP – takes out a small phial. She keeps her eyes on PHILIP, then suddenly leans forward and empties the phial into his cup of tea. She straightens up and closes her handbag.

PHILIP: I'm sorry about that.

HELEN: (*Quietly*) You know who telephoned me this afternoon, don't you?

PHILIP: Yes.

HELEN: Who was it?

PHILIP: A man called David Jefferies; he used to be an actor – we thought he might impersonate your brother better than anyone else.

HELEN: 'We'?

PHILIP: Major Harris, Inspector Hilton …

169

HELEN: What was the point?

PHILIP: Would you have come here this afternoon if you hadn't have been doubtful about Martin?

HELEN: (*A moment*) Is Martin dead?

PHILIP: (*Shaking his head*) He's in St Matthew's Hospital.

HELEN: (*Angry*) Then why did you lie to me last night?

PHILIP: Harris asked me to. Besides, it made a nice change – you've usually done the lying, Helen.

HELEN looks at PHILIP; hesitates, picks up her cup of tea.

HELEN: You said this morning, on the telephone, there was a question you wanted to ask me.

PHILIP: (*Picking up his cup of tea*) Yes.

HELEN: What was it?

PHILIP: (*Suddenly; putting down his cup*) How did you get like this? What started it? What – what happens to a person?

HELEN: Hasn't Martin told you?

PHILIP: I haven't seen Martin; no one's allowed to see him, except his wife.

HELEN: (*Bitterly; revealing a different side to her personality*) His wife! That stupid, ignorant, little fool! If Martin hadn't fallen head over heels in love with her this would never have happened.

PHILIP: (*Quietly*) Well, it did happen – thank God!

HELEN: (*Putting down her cup of tea*) Tell me, just as a matter of curiosity, when did you first suspect me?

PHILIP: The day I found the lucky charm,

HELEN: (*Nodding*) Yes, that was a piece of bad luck; I only discovered it was missing on the way back to town. I daren't return to the houseboat for it.

PHILIP: Why did you kill Rice – because of the letter?

170

HELEN: Yes. He told Kesner I wasn't co-operating. It
            was a lie – a deliberate lie. I couldn't find
            Martin – I'd been trying to find him for weeks.
            That's why I went to see Ruth that night. I
            thought she might have heard from him.

PHILIP: Martin has more sense than to contact Ruth.
            He knew the moment he did that her life would
            be in danger.

HELEN: Her life was already in danger. You saved her
            that night, you know that, don't you?

PHILIP: Yes.

HELEN: (*Touching her cup; smiling, as if to herself*) Do
            you remember when you first saw Martin – the
            night you brought me the note?

PHILIP: Yes.

HELEN: Do you know what really happened that night?

PHILIP: (*Nodding*) I made a mistake.

HELEN: (*Puzzled*) What do you mean?

PHILIP: I telephoned you from the restaurant. I told you
            that I'd seen Martin and that I was bringing you
            a letter from him. When I got to your flat you'd
            already written another letter; you had a
            convenient fainting fit and switched the letters
            while I was getting you a glass of brandy.

HELEN: Go on …

PHILIP: The letter you showed me, the letter that was
            supposed to have been written by Martin, put
            all the blame on Ruth. But in actual fact the
            letter that Martin wrote, the real letter, was
            quite different …

HELEN: How do you know?

PHILIP: I've seen it.

HELEN: (*Surprised*) You've seen it?

PHILIP: Yes.

171

HELEN: But that's impossible!
PHILIP: Oh, no. Shall I read it to you? (*He takes a note from his pocket; reads:*) 'Dear Helen … I think it's about time we stopped playing cat and mouse. Meet me tomorrow night at Auberge d'Armaille, ten o'clock. I warn you, Helen – don't bring any of your friends … Martin' … (*Looking up*) That's when Martin really made the appointment. The phone call you received was a fake, just for my benefit.

HELEN takes the note out of PHILIP's hand and looks at it.

HELEN: (*Tensely*) Where did you get this from?
PHILIP: Major Harris.
HELEN: But how did he –?
PHILIP: Your flat was searched – remember?
HELEN: Your friend Harris seems to have thought of everything!
PHILIP: Not everything. I've had a few bright ideas myself. (*He picks up his cup of tea*) However, there's one thing I don't understand.
HELEN: (*Watching him*) Well?
PHILIP: Why did you tell Harris about Kesner – if you hadn't have done that I should have gone to Berlin.
HELEN: And delivered Rice's letter? That's not what I wanted …
PHILIP: (*Nodding*) I see.

A moment.

HELEN: How bad is Martin?
PHILIP: Pretty bad. But he'll get better.
HELEN: Has he made a statement?
PHILIP: I believe so. The police raided a house this morning and picked up some of your friends.

This registers with HELEN; she looks worried. There is a pause. PHILIP looks at the cup of tea; raises it nearer his mouth. He stops. He looks at HELEN, over the cup. HELEN watches him, waiting for him to drink. A long pause.

PHILIP: I'm afraid you overlooked the family motto, Miss Teckman. (*He smiles, leans forward and pours the contents of the cup into a basin on the trolley*) Take no chances, Chance!

HELEN is angry; she rises. Suddenly, quickly, she turns towards the alcove. DETECTIVE-INSPECTOR HILTON and MAJOR HARRIS are standing in the doorway. HILTON crosses to HELEN.

HILTON: Hello, Miss Teckman. We've been hearing quite a lot about you this afternoon. Your colleagues can certainly talk!

HARRIS: (*Crossing the room; to PHILIP*) Where's the recorder?

PHILIP: It's in the bedroom.

HELEN looks at PHILIP; she is tense; frightened.

CUT TO: The recording machine in the bedroom. It is in action, the tape-wheels revolving.

CUT TO: The Golden Arrow at Victoria Station.

PHILIP arrives complete with a PORTER carrying suitcases etc. MAURICE MILLER walks by his side. They enter the train. A uniformed, Golden Arrow attendant salutes them as they do so.

CUT TO: The interior of the train.

PHILIP takes off his hat and coat. He sits in his reserved seat. There is a vacant seat next to him which MAURICE MILLER drops into.

PHILIP: It's jolly nice of you to see me off, Maurice.

173

MILLER: Not at all, old boy. I wish I was coming with you.

PHILIP: Well – why not?

MILLER: Too much work, Philip. Far too much.

PHILIP: Maurice, one of these days you'll be the richest man in the cemetery.

MILLER smiles.

PHILIP: Well, another forty-eight hours and I shall be in the South of France, thank goodness.

MILLER: The sunny place for shady people.

PHILIP: (*Frowning*) Yes.

MILLER: (*Noticing PHILIP's reaction to the remark*) What is it?

PHILIP: Oh, nothing.

MILLER: Well, why the frown?

PHILIP: Someone else once made that remark to me, that's all.

MILLER: I didn't think it was original.

PHILIP: (*Quietly*) It was Helen Teckman.

MILLER: Oh, I see.

A slight pause.

MILLER: Philip, we've known one another a very long time, haven't we?

PHILIP: A very long time, old boy.

MILLER: Do you mind if I ask you a rather personal question?

PHILIP: Don't be silly …

MILLER: Were you in love with Helen Teckman?

PHILIP: (*A moment; shaking his head*) No. It was a jolly near thing, but I wasn't in love with her. (*Smiling*) As a matter of fact, Maurice, I'll let you into a secret – a rather terrifying one. I don't fall in love with people, I fall in love with places.

MILLER: Isn't that rather unsatisfactory? Places change.

174

PHILIP: So do people; and you can't do anything about it. You can always find a new place to go to.

MILLER: Philip, you're a cynic.

PHILIP: So? You surprise me! (*Laughing*) Good gracious, you've been publishing my books for years and you've only just discovered that!

MILLER: I saw Barbara Jefferies last night.

PHILIP: Oh, did you? What does she look like?

MILLER: Well, she's lost a certain amount of weight, but she doesn't look at all bad. She's made a   surprising recovery.

PHILIP: She has indeed. Did you talk to her about the biography?

MILLER: Yes, she's going to write it. I hope you don't   mind, Philip?

PHILIP: My dear fellow, I'm delighted!

MILLER: I feel I've messed you about rather badly.

PHILIP: (*Pulling MILLER's leg*) I'm an author – you're a publisher. It's inevitable.

MILLER: You don't seriously call yourself an author, do you? Four books in sixteen years?

PHILIP: Now don't start on that!

MILLER laughs and rises.

MILLER: (*Shaking hands*) Goodbye, Philip! Have a good time! Give my love to Paris!

PHILIP: I will indeed! Oh, and if you feel like doing me a good turn …

MILLER: Yes?

PHILIP: Bring out a cheap edition of "Destiny At Dawn".

MILLER: (*Laughing*) Now don't you start on that!

PHILIP laughs. MAURICE waves to him.

MILLER: Goodbye!

MAURICE goes. PHILIP rises; re-arranges himself; makes himself comfortable. He is in the process of doing this when

LYDIA *arrives. She is very good looking; sophisticated. She carries a book, magazine, newspapers, under her arm. There is a porter with her, and he arranges her luggage; she tips him and takes the vacant seat next to* PHILIP. *The porter leaves.* LYDIA *looks at* PHILIP *and smiles. He smiles at her. She makes herself comfortable; puts down the newspapers and magazines; opens her book. We see the title is "Destiny At Dawn", and the photograph of* PHILIP *on the back of the jacket.* PHILIP *is now looking out of the window; he hasn't noticed the book. He turns; notices that the girl is reading; glances at the book; turns away. He suddenly realises what she is reading and stares at the book again. He is staggered. The girl looks up and smiles.*

LYDIA: (*Pleasantly*) Have you read it?

PHILIP: (*Staggered*) Yes, I have – as a matter of fact.

LYDIA: It's awfully good.

PHILIP: (*Apprehensively*) Do you think so?

LYDIA: Terribly good.

PHILIP: You don't think it's a silly story?

LYDIA: Of course not!

PHILIP: And not pretentious in any way?

LYDIA: Not in the slightest.

PHILIP: (*A sigh of relief*) Oh!

LYDIA: You sound relieved?

PHILIP: I am.

LYDIA *looks puzzled; glances down at the book, notices the photograph of* PHILIP, *suddenly looks up at him. She is very surprised.*

LYDIA: Good gracious! Are you Philip Chance?

PHILIP: Me?

LYDIA: Yes.

PHILIP: Why – (*Suddenly*) Why, no! What makes you think so?

176

LYDIA:	(*Looking at the photograph*) This photograph – it's terribly like you.
PHILIP:	He's – he's my brother.
LYDIA:	Oh. (*Smiling*) Oh, I see. (*Looking at PHILIP*) My word, you are alike!
PHILIP:	We're both the same age.
LYDIA:	Oh.
PHILIP:	(*Enjoying himself*) Twins.
LYDIA:	Ah – that explains it.
PHILIP:	I thought it would.
LYDIA:	Well, you brother's a very good writer, Mr Chance.
PHILIP:	Thank you.
LYDIA:	Do you write novels?
PHILIP:	(*Smiling; moving closer to LYDIA*) Not if I can possibly help it! Strictly the South of France type, that's me!

PHILIP looks at LYDIA and smiles. She laughs. PHILIP starts laughing too.

THE END

Alvin Rakoff, aged 93, director of the tv serial *The Teckman Biography* is interviewed by renowned Francis Durbridge expert, **Dr Georg Pagitz,** January 2020.

GP: You were very young when you got the job of directing *The Teckman Biography* – you were 26 years old. How did this come about?

AR: I was just beginning to make a name for myself. I'd come over from Canada – the Canadian Broadcasting Company had sent me over (they weren't broadcasting television yet in Canada), to see what the BBC who started television were doing. So I came over for three months ostensibly, in 1952. And so by the time we get to 1953 when this is I'd made a few productions and was beginning to make a name for myself and Francis Durbridge wanted a change of his usual producer and director. So he asked the BBC if they could use this new guy – me! I read the scripts, heard of Francis Durbridge and so I said "Yes, ok" so that's the way it was. It was really Francis who made the change more than me. And Michael Barry who was the head of BBC Drama at that time was the one who put us together.

GP: Had you already heard of Francis Durbridge before?

AR: Oh yes. He was a great writer who was well-known for his radio serials about Paul Temple which began long before he started writing for television.

GP: Yes, he wrote his first Paul Temple serial in 1938.

AR: You've got to remember it was a different atmosphere completely then. When I told people at the BBC that I was interested and wanted to do television they kept saying "Don't do television – do radio – because

179

television is going to disappear tomorrow. It's only a temporary thing." Francis Durbridge was a very much respected radio writer and I was this young and very inexperienced television director.

GP: It must have been a big honour for you to be asked to do *The Teckman Biography* serial.

AR: It was.

GP: It was Patrick Barr who played the lead character, Philip Chance.

AR: I'd worked with Patrick before when I wasn't even a director – I was producing for the BBC. The first big job I had at the BBC was a television adaptation of an American novel called *The Troubled Air*. Patrick played the lead in that. That was when I first met Patrick Barr and then I cast him in *The Teckman Biography*. I liked the way he worked for his honesty.

GP: Who was responsible for the casting of *The Teckman Biography*?

AR: It was me. Remember, in those days the director was also the producer. Francis was interested but I don't even know if I checked every cast member with him – I just told him who I was going to cast in which role and that was that. He had no responsibility or desire to be anyway involved directly with the casting. He was a writer and he was just interested in who I was going to use.

GP: Each episode of *The Teckman Biography* went out live, didn't they?

AR: Of course. Everything was live – there was no way of recording until the sixties.

GP: Can you explain how that worked? About the rehearsal process …

AR: The way we worked was that we rehearsed for five days and then we had one day in the studio. On Saturday morning, with the rehearsed cast, I would go into Alexandra Palace studios, which was the first public broadcasting studios in the world, and I would do a camera rehearsal and then it would go out in the evening at about 8 o'clock which was a very popular timeslot for a television serial. They were called serials because they were limited to so many episodes. This was limited to six episodes. I must tell you, Alexandra Palace was beyond your imagination. There was only one camera out of the four that moved – and that camera was on a platform on bicycle wheels, and it was a big, cumbersome movement, and the viewfinder on the cameras on the floor was upside down – the picture was upside down! Also, the cameras were so cumbersome and heavy and big that you couldn't get close to the actors and I was a young director and I wanted my close-ups to be big close-ups like they are today. In those days you were lucky if you got from below the shoulders to above the head, so I would say "No, that's not close enough" and in the last episode of *The Teckman Biography* I wanted the final scene to have really big close-ups, so the actors had to play it, not to each other, although it was a very intimate and powerful scene, they had to play it to the camera so they could walk right up to the camera and be closer. You can imagine for an emotional scene how difficult that would be for two actors to do, you know, saying "I love you" "I hate you!" to a camera is very difficult.

GP: Where were the location scenes shot?

AR: In addition to the studio and doing live television there were scenes that had to be shot on film. There was a scene I remember where the detectives had to run across a bridge over the Thames – we used a bridge outside of London in a town called Datchet – it was Datchet Bridge we used. There were about two or three minutes of filming in each episode although some episodes didn't have any. The episodes were half an hour long and there were no commercial breaks in those days and I would say at least twenty-five minutes of each episode was done in the studio.

GP: So you worked on it for six weeks really for the Saturday night transmission of the episode.

AR: Of course I worked on it before the six weeks as I had to do the casting, the sets, etc etc. I would say it was one or two months before the rehearsals started, then six weeks of rehearsals and transmission and then the clearing up period was only a day or two after.

GP: Did you have the entire script for all six episodes or did the actors, for example, only get the script for each episode?

AR: Francis would never give anybody the final script, because what he did, as he admitted to me later, is that he watched each episode and he watched the actors developing their characters and then he picked the actor who was least likely to be suspicious to the audience and he made them the guilty person. He was so adroit at making changes and making the script fit. Most writers would plan the whole thing in advance but we didn't get the final script until a few days before the final week so in the penultimate week the cast would say "Who did it?" and I would say, "I don't know – Francis will tell me."

GP: So even you didn't know before the sixth episode?

AR: No, I didn't know until the end of the fifth week of rehearsals. I think the weekend before we began the final week Francis put the script in my hand and then I knew. He must have had some thoughts at the beginning but he admitted that that was the way he liked to work. He didn't like to finalise anything until he had seen how the cast were working and who would be the least suspected. He was a very unique writer.

GP: The theme music was called *The Shadow Waltz*. Was this your idea?

AR: Yes, completely. It wasn't the sort of thing Francis would be involved in. I think the BBC had a record library to help producers find music. I think I told the guy in charge what I wanted and he came up with *The Shadow Waltz*. He came up with several pieces of music. I said I wanted nothing too obvious because in those days everybody was using very heavy-handed music – you know – boom, boom, boom – every time something dramatic was going to happen. I wanted a change from all that. I wanted to change a lot of things. So he played this light waltz and I said "That's it! That's what we're using."

GP: After the tv production there was a production which adapted the story for the big screen. Do you know that film – *The Teckman Mystery*?

AR: Yes, and it was very upsetting to me because they gave it to a camera woman, Wendy Toye, to direct the film and I felt that was wrong, I felt she was wrong, she hadn't my experience as a director. I don't know why Korda gave it to her and not to me. Korda was a fan of the series from the beginning although he never contacted me but he went into the office after the first episode at British Lion, Shepperton, and spoke to his assistant about the programme. I was contacted by the assistant but never got contacted by Mr Korda directly, I never spoke to him directly and then I heard that Wendy Toye had been made the director and considering all the work I had done I found it very upsetting. And I still find it upsetting. I still think it was wrong. All Wendy Toye did was try to imitate the television version and I strongly feel that there's a huge difference between shooting something for the sitting room and something for the cinema. It wasn't well directed, I think, anybody looking at it will see it was very dull direction.

GP: This is what I thought when I recently watched it. It's like a tv production and not like a film for the big screen.

AR: Exactly.

GP: There are two locations – the flat of the author and the flat of Teckman's sister – and there are always people coming in and going out. It's like a stage play. But, however, *The Shadow Waltz* is used in the credits.

AR: They used *The Shadow Waltz* as well? That shows how much they stole from me. In every way it was wrong. It was wrong morally and creatively. If I'd directed the film I think I would have asked Francis to make certain changes to make it more suitable for the big screen – more outside scenes, exteriors in different parts of the world. I wanted to make it more cinematic and I was aware, arriving as a foreigner, how wonderful England was as a backdrop for a picture.

GP: However, in the film, there is the final scene shot on Tower Bridge and at the Tower of London which wasn't in the tv production.

AR: I went to see the film but I walked out because I found it very upsetting. I felt they were just imitating everything I did. And I told Francis Durbridge, we discussed it, "It's a reproduction of the television," I said.

GP: There was Peter Coke in the production who a few months later got the role of Paul Temple on the radio.

AR: I don't remember using Peter Coke but if I did use him it was probably because Francis asked me to use him – that's the way he would have got the job. He was not an outstanding television actor in any way or a film actor.

GP: And before each episode was transmitted was there somebody who summarised what had already happened because in the *Radio Times* you didn't find a word about what had happened? Was there an announcer who summarised the last episode?

AR: No, if the viewers hadn't seen the last episode it was too bad.

GP: Do you remember what was the reaction of the audience?

AR: The reaction was huge! Huge! To this day the British Film Institute have copies of the publicity which was tremendous. The audience was huge and it built up each week. We had a Saturday night effect on cinemas throughout Britain. It was tremendous. That's why Korda made a film of it because he thought he could capitalise on that. There was a big critical reaction!

GP: After this production you didn't return to Francis Durbridge. You made lots of other productions for tv and then the cinema.

AR: That's right. I was about to do Francis's next serial *Portrait of Alison*, I agreed with the BBC that I would do the serial that followed, but I became ill. I was supposed to do that but I had a lung collapse which was pretty serious. I was rushed to hospital, they operated on it and it put me out of action for a month. So somebody else had to do it and I never did any more with Francis Durbridge though we talked about it.

GP: Do you have any recollections about how Francis Durbridge was as a man – as a person?

AR: He was very pleasant. He was a very pleasant man. A very practical, very down to earth, there was no pretensions or 'side' as they say here in England. There was nothing grand about him. He liked his job, he knew he could write, he knew he had big audiences and he was very good for a young, up and coming director to work with at the time. The thing that you must remember, this is the difference between live television – it was awful! There was the chance of a camera breaking down, an actor breaking down or forgetting their words or moving to the wrong place – the horrors

186

of live television can only be remembered by those that did it and we're disappearing quickly.

Press Pack

… press cuttings about *The Teckman Mystery* – the film version of *The Teckman Biography*

A Lethal Life-Story by Gerald Bowman

After her magnificent work in Shakespeare and Shaw, in Chekov and T.S. Eliot, Margaret Leighton is now to appear in Durbridge.

The Teckman Biography, a successful tv serial by Francis ("Paul Temple") Durbridge, is being brought to the screen at Shepperton Studios by Wendy Toye, the dancer-producer-director, who has made everything from Cochran shows to an Academy Award film (her first, *The Stranger Left No Card*) at the Cannes Festival last year.

John Justin and Roland Culver have joined the cast – straight from the stage next door, where they have been making *The Man Who Loved Redheads*, with Moira Shearer. Margaret, herself, has had only to walk across a corridor from the set where she had been making *The Constant Husband* with Rex Harrison.

This is a straightforward thriller, as TV viewers already know. An author, writing the life-story of a test pilot who has crashed, finds that he runs into a succession of "accidents." Robbery and murder become normal everyday incidents around him.

At the Gaumont

Already heralded in advance as a top-flight murder mystery – as it should be, coming from the pen of radio's master mysterious, Francis Durbridge – *The Teckman Mystery*, which is showing at the Gaumont Cinema, Burton, for the rest of the week, has a combination of delicate touches of comedy, high-speed action and an absorbing plot.

The story is of Philip Chance, a young and successful author who is given the job of writing the biography of Martin Teckman, an airman who was killed while testing a secret jet prototype in the air. He soon discovers a number of strange people who appear to be equally interested in the dead airman, and in alliance with the dead man's beautiful sister, he unravels the mystery.

Deft comedy touches, in the best tradition of the screen master filmmakers, appear throughout the film and often give added point to the story, proving once again that in Wendy Toye Britain has one of the most talented women film directors.

Outstanding acting from the beautiful Margaret Leighton, a rugged performance from John Justin as the dogged author, and fine portrayals from Roland Culver and Michael Medwin, round off the highly-creditable and thoroughly entertaining mystery thriller.

Burton Daily Mail

The Teckman Mystery
This is a sprightly British whodunnit concerning current cold-war conventions, with a novelist commissioned to write the biography of a mysterious test pilot dogged by a succession of Iron Curtain agents. There are several corpses and a plethora of red herrings. There are some slick, lightweight performances from leads who deal easily with breezy dialogue, and some engaging support cameos. There is brisk direction and lively camera work on familiar London settings. This is clean-cut, fast-moving family entertainment for any situation.

As is the case with many thrillers, this story contains a number of quite startling improbabilities. However, director Wendy Toye gives her audience no chance to ponder on these as she piles incident on incident to keep the action moving. Light handling of character and plenty of comedy keeps the blood-splattered story from seeming too horrific, and the climax is a refreshingly new variant of the inevitable chase sequence.

Today's Cinema

The Teckman Mystery *(contains spoilers)*
If you have a tv set you will hardly be baffled by *The Teckman Mystery* unless you missed the last instalment of *The Teckman Biography*, the Alexandra Palace serial on which it is based.

But even if you know the solution I still think you will find this an intriguing, well-acted, highly entertaining spy story.

Martin Teckman is a test pilot who has disappeared while flying a secret plane, the F109.

John Justin, a young novelist is commissioned to write his biography and so many alarming things happen to him as a result that it is clear he will stick to fiction in future.

A sinister-looking gent with a Central European accent offers him a large sum of money to go to Berlin and write some articles for an American magazine that doesn't exist.

And when he calls at a young woman's apartment in answer to a strange telephone call he finds Margaret Leighton waiting behind a curtain with a gun.

Despite the gun, this seemed to me to be adequate compensation for all the rest. For Miss Leighton is the most elegant charmer in British films.

She is Teckman's sister. Is her brother really dead? Did the F109 really disintegrate in mid-air? Or did Teckman really fly it to a foreign country anxious to know its secrets?

Like *To Dorothy A Son* this film was directed by a woman – former ballet dancer Wendy Toye.

Films are made primarily to appeal to women. Why, then, have so few made their mark as directors?

"It has taken a long time to persuade men to give us the opportunity," says Muriel Box.

"Perhaps they thought we couldn't do it," says Wendy Toye who looks much too fragile and feminine to have been responsible for anything as tough as *The Teckman Mystery*.

But I wish she hadn't included that scene in which a young airman says "One thing about flying – up there you can see things clearly."

How many times have you heard that line before? One day I am going to write a film script about a deep sea diver who says "One thing about diving – down there you can hardly see anything at all."

The Star